Spywatch

THE NOVEL

Derek Farmer

Published by BBC Educational Publishing,
a division of BBC Education,
BBC White City,
201 Wood Lane,
London W12 7TS

First published 1995
Reprinted 1995, 1997, 1999 and 2001
© Derek Farmer/BBC Education, 1995

The moral right of the author has been asserted.

Illustrations © Ray and Corinne Burrows, 1995
Cover photo © John Jefford/BBC Education, 1995
Text edited by Debbie Reid
Cover and book design by Claire Robertson

ISBN: 0 563 37280 X

Set in Stone Informal

Printed in England by Clays Ltd, St Ives plc

Contents

Glossary		4
1	Sent away	5
2	Grainger danger	17
3	Spies all around	29
4	Trouble for Mary	42
5	The poster comes to life	56
6	Bombs in the country	70
7	Surprise	82
8	The pilot	94
9	The secret quarry	104
10	Captured	115

Glossary

black market
illegal buying and selling of goods

evacuee
person who is moved from a place of danger to safety

G.I.
soldier of the US army

Jerry
nickname for German soldier

P.O.W.
prisoner of war

P.X. shop
shop on soldier's camp

saboteur
person who deliberately destroys something

spiv
person who makes a living from dishonest dealings

wireless
a radio

SENT AWAY

Norman Starkey stepped out of the air raid shelter and looked around.

It was wartime. Planes were bombing the cities. Lots of children had been sent away to stay with people in the countryside. It was safer there. Evacuees they were called.

Most of Norman's friends had gone. But not Norman. He didn't want to go. He wanted to stay behind with his mother. In the end, she let him.

The bombs had been closer than usual that night. Everywhere Norman looked there were buildings still burning.

Norman wandered through the battered streets. The pavements were strewn with shattered glass and rubble.

Norman turned on to the road where he lived. Most of the houses were still standing. But, at the far end, a crowd was gathered around an ambulance.

Norman ran to see what was happening, As he got there, his next door neighbour, Mrs Thompson, was being stretchered into the ambulance. She was lucky to be alive. She always refused to go to the air raid shelter and the house had received a direct hit.

There was a hole in the ground where Mrs Thompson's house used to be. Most of Norman's house had been destroyed with it.

Norman's mother, Mrs Starkey, was staring at the wreckage.

She turned to Norman. Her eyes were red from crying. "Norman!" she said. "It's just too dangerous here. You've got to go."

Norman argued and pleaded, but Mrs Starkey was determined. This time, there was no persuading her.

So that afternoon, Norman was put on a train with a label round his neck and sent away to the countryside. It was like a foreign land to him.

———————◆———————

Mr Jenkins was waiting for Norman at the other end. Mr Jenkins was the village postman, but he also had the job of finding places for the city children to live.

"Norman Starkey, eh?" Mr Jenkins checked the label pinned to Norman's coat. "You come with me. I've got a nice new home waiting for you."

Mr Jenkins put Norman in the back of his car. A girl was already there. Hunched up in one corner.

"This is Mary Parker," said Mr Jenkins. "She's an evacuee as well."

Mary was about the same age as Norman. She was wearing her school uniform. Her hands were folded in her lap. She was staring down at them. She didn't even look up when Norman got into the car.

Norman knew how she felt. Lonely and scared.
Too lonely to talk.

The car pulled out of the station yard and turned
along the main street. Minutes later, they had left the
village and were out in the country.

Norman had never seen anything like it before.
Mile after mile of emptiness. Fields, hedges and trees,
and more fields.

"How do you like it in the country then?" Mr Jenkins
said over his shoulder.

Norman glared out the window. "Is this all there is?"
He wasn't impressed. It was like one enormous park –
without the swings!

"You'll soon get used to it," said Mr Jenkins.

Norman slumped against the side of the car. He'd
never get used to it. He didn't want to get used to it.
He wanted to go home. And the sooner the better.

"Anybody like chocolate?" Mr Jenkins called out.

Norman sat up and took notice. He loved chocolate.
And he was starving hungry. "I love chocolate," he said.

Mr Jenkins nodded. "So do I. They had some in the
village shop a couple of months ago."

Norman sighed. It looked as though there was no
more chocolate in the countryside than there was in the
city. And he was still starving.

Then Mary touched his arm. She was holding a bar
of chocolate. A whole bar of chocolate. She broke it in
two and passed one half to Norman.

Norman couldn't believe it. A total stranger was giving him half her chocolate. It was unheard of. He grabbed it quickly before she could change her mind. He snapped off a piece and popped it in his mouth. Mary put the rest back in her pocket.

Mr Jenkins brought the car to a stop and switched off the engine. "Here we are then," he said. "Westbourne Hall. Your new home – I hope!" he muttered as he climbed out.

Westbourne Hall was a large country house which had seen better days. It was full of statues and stuffed animals. Peacocks strutted in the grounds. It had at least thirty bedrooms and once would have been packed with family and servants. Now only two people lived there, Phillip Grainger and his housekeeper, Miss Millington.

Phillip Grainger was not pleased to see them. He was a tall, thin man with angry eyes. He listened impatiently while Jenkins told him why Norman and Mary were there. Then he stopped him with a wave of the hand.

"What do you think I'm running here, Jenkins? A Children's Home?" he sneered.

"They'll be no trouble, Mr Grainger," Jenkins replied. "You'll hardly know they're here, sir."

"That's because they won't be here," Grainger told him. "I'm much too busy to fool about with evacuees. Get them out of here."

Jenkins sighed. "In that case, sir, I'm going to have to report you to the authorities."

"Hang on a minute." Grainger had to be careful. He could be in trouble if he refused to take in evacuees. He decided to do a deal.

"I'll take one of them," he said. "The girl."

Jenkins thought it over. One was better than none. And it was best not to force people if you could help it.

"Is something wrong?" Miss Millington was on her way down the stairs.

"No, it's all sorted out," Grainger said. "Mr Jenkins has brought us an evacuee."

"Evacuee?" Miss Millington was a small, dark woman with an icy glare that she turned on Jenkins. "But we're not used to looking after children."

"Don't worry, Miss Millington," said Jenkins. He was already leaving. "Mary Parker's her name. She's a good girl. She won't bite." Jenkins was hurrying Norman back to the car. He wanted to get away before Grainger changed his mind. "Now, son," he said. "What are we going to do with you?"

It was late and Jenkins still had to find somewhere for Norman to sleep. He decided to take a chance on Wells Farm.

➤◆◄

Wells Farm was only a short drive from Westbourne Hall. It was the home of Mrs Amy Hobbs. Mrs Hobbs was a kind-hearted old lady who was always ready to help. The problem was Mr Jenkins had already left an evacuee there earlier in the day.

Mr Jenkins needn't have worried. Mrs Hobbs took one look at Norman and pulled him inside. "Let's get him fed," she said. "Before he wastes away."

She gave Norman a big bowl of soup and a hunk of home-baked bread. Then she sat down to listen to Mr Jenkins' story.

"So Mr High and Mighty Grainger wouldn't have him then?" she said when she heard what had happened at Westbourne Hall.

"Didn't want him or the girl," said Jenkins.

"I knew he was no good the day he arrived," said Mrs Hobbs. "Money! That's all that one's interested in."

Mr Jenkins nodded.

"More soup, Norman?" asked Mrs Hobbs.

"Can I have more bread as well?"

Mrs Hobbs smiled. "You can. But then it's straight to bed, mind."

⟶➤◆⟵

At Westbourne Hall, Miss Millington had taken Mary straight up to one of the empty bedrooms and left her there.

Mary didn't know what to do. She started to unpack. It didn't take long. She didn't have much.

Finally, she was left with the half bar of chocolate and a pound note that her mother had given her. She put them under her pillow. They would be safe there.

Downstairs, Miss Millington was in a rage. "What's the idea of having that girl here?" she shouted at Grainger.

Grainger shrugged. "He said he'd report us to the authorities if I refused. Do you want them up here poking their noses in?"

"So instead we've got that girl snooping around all the time!" Millington snapped.

Grainger tried to calm things down. "You can take care of her all right," he said. "She's just a kid."

Millington glared at him. She would just have to make sure that Mary was no trouble and didn't go snooping around at night.

<hr/>

Mrs Hobbs opened the door to the bedroom. "No noise, mind," she whispered. "Don't want to wake Dennis, do we?"

Norman was puzzled. "Who is Dennis, Mrs Hobbs?"

"Call me Aunty Amy," Mrs Hobbs told him. "Dennis is my other evacuee. He'll be fast asleep in bed now."

But he wasn't. There was nobody in the bed.

"Good Lord!" said Amy. "He's disappeared!"

Amy pulled open the wardrobe door and looked inside. Dennis wasn't there.

"The window!" said Amy. "He must've got out through the window."

But Norman had spotted something. A foot was sticking out from under the bed. Amy bent down and grabbed it. She pulled. A boy slid out. An untidy-looking boy who was still half-asleep. It was Dennis Sealey. Dennis sat up and rubbed his eyes.

"What's the idea sleeping under the bed?" Amy demanded.

"That's where I sleep at home," Dennis yawned. "Bombs can't get you there."

Amy shook her head. "We don't have bombs here," she told Dennis. "So you don't have to be scared."

"Who said I was scared?"

"Nobody," Amy smiled. "You're both very brave boys, I'm sure."

———————◆◗●◖◆———————

"Right! Time we had a little chat."

Mary was sitting up in bed while Miss Millington told her the rules of the house. The rules were simple. Whatever Miss Millington said, Mary had to do.

"Understand?" Millington asked her.

Mary understood.

But that wasn't all.

"By the way," Miss Millington added on her way out. "You're not afraid of ghosts, are you?"

Mary's eyes opened wide.

"An old house like this is bound to have one or two, isn't it?" said Millington. "You might hear odd noises in the night. But you'll be all right as long as you stay in your room. And don't go wandering round the house."

It sounded more like a threat than advice.

Millington switched off the light and shut the door. Mary didn't dare move. She just sat in the dark and listened for ghosts.

———⟫●⟪———

Norman and Dennis sat side by side in the big double bed. They were trying to be brave but Amy could see there was something wrong. She had an idea.

"I just remembered," she said. "I've got something for you."

Amy pulled open a drawer and took out a torch and a small telescope. She threw them on to the bed. Norman and Dennis grabbed them.

"Share them," said Amy. "They used to be my boy's. He's got army ones now."

Amy closed the door. Norman and Dennis clutched their new things to them as they settled down to sleep.

Already they were starting to feel better about being away from home. They were the lucky ones.

———❖———

At Westbourne Hall, Mary was lying wide-awake in the dark. It wasn't the thought of ghosts that was keeping her awake. It was the thought of Grainger and Miss Millington. Mary knew that she was never going to be happy with those two. She turned over and tried to sleep. But Millington's words just kept going round and round in her head.

———❖———

Norman and Dennis were fast asleep. A sudden noise cut through the air. Norman sat bolt-upright. He couldn't believe it. Something was tapping at the window! Trying to get in.

But that wasn't possible. Was it? Perhaps he'd dreamt it.

But there it was again. A sharp "tap, tap, tap" against the glass.

There was no mistaking it this time. Norman grabbed Dennis and shook him.

"Dennis! Wake up!" he said. "There's something at the window."

GRAINGER DANGER

Dennis sat up. Suddenly he was wide awake.
Listening.

Silence. Then the tapping again. Louder this time.
Norman and Dennis stared at the window. The curtain
flapped gently in the breeze. Behind it, a ghostly
shadow danced from side to side.

Tap! Tap! Tap!

"Have a look," Dennis gulped.

"Me?" Norman didn't want to look, but Dennis was
daring him. And Norman didn't want Dennis to think
he was scared.

He grabbed the curtain. Took a deep breath and
pulled it to one side. There was nothing there.

Then, slowly, the end of a broom appeared from
below and clattered against the window pane. The
broom was tied to a long stick.

Somebody was on the other end of that stick. But who?

Norman and Dennis looked out of the window. A
girl was standing in the front garden, waving the stick
from side to side. She was wearing a nightdress and a
wicked grin.

"Not scared, are you?" she hissed. "I thought you townies weren't scared of anything."

Norman and Dennis fell back from the window.

"Night, night. Sleep tight. Only hope the bugs don't bite," chanted the girl. "See you in the morning."

"Who's that then?" said Norman.

Dennis shrugged. "Whoever it is – I don't like her."

———⟫●⟪———

The next morning, Amy sat Norman and Dennis at the kitchen table and put plates crammed with bacon and eggs in front of them.

The two boys just stared. They hadn't seen anything like it since the beginning of the war. In the cities, bacon was an occasional treat, and real eggs were hard to get.

Amy was puzzled. "Not hungry?" she asked.

Dennis pointed at the fried eggs. "Please, Aunty Amy," he said. "Are they eggs?"

Amy nodded. " Of course they are. Don't you like fried eggs?"

Dennis didn't know. He hadn't had one for so long. "We only have powdered eggs at home."

Amy smiled at him. She'd forgotten that there was a shortage of eggs. Living on a farm meant that there was always plenty of fresh food.

"Try these," she said. "You'll like them."

Norman and Dennis grabbed their knives and forks and prepared to tuck in. But before they could get so much as a mouthful, the stairs door opened and there stood the girl.

She was dressed now. But she still had the same wicked grin.

"And about time too, madam," Amy scolded. "Anybody would think you'd been up half the night."

The grin on the girl's face grew even broader. She knew something that Amy didn't.

"This is my granddaughter, Polly," Amy told the boys. "Hurry up and clear your plates and she'll show you what's what and where's where."

Dennis and Norman looked at each other in despair. Not only were they stuck with a girl, but she was going to be in charge of them.

———⇒●⇐———

At Westbourne Hall, Mary was given bread and margarine for breakfast.

"Let's get one thing straight," Miss Millington told her. "This is not a holiday." She thrust an apron at Mary. "Put that on," she said.

Millington munched her toast and marmalade while Mary put the apron on. It was much too big for her. She felt silly in it. But she said nothing.

Millington took another mouthful of toast.

"You don't expect to live here for nothing, do you?" she demanded. "After all, we didn't ask you to come. You can work for your keep."

Millington got up. "Well don't just stand there," she said to Mary. "Clear the table."

Mary could see she was in for a hard time. Millington was out to make her life a misery. But Mary wouldn't give in, and she'd never let Millington see that she was upset.

Norman and Dennis were upset. They stood at the gate at the end of the path and stared nervously across the farmyard.

Polly was waiting impatiently. "Are you going to stand there all day?" she called out.

Norman and Dennis scowled. They didn't need anybody to show them round. Especially that girl. But Amy had told them to go with Polly so that was what they had to do, like it or not.

Norman stepped out into the farmyard. There was a horrible squelching sound. He looked down. His foot was in the middle of an enormous cow-pat.

The grin was back on Polly's face. "That's the first thing you townies have to learn," she said. "Watch where you're putting your big feet. You never know when you might tread on an unexploded cow-pat."

Polly flounced off across the yard. Now she was two up on the boys, and they knew it.

"We'll get her for that," Dennis whispered.

But Polly wasn't going to be easy to get. Neither Norman nor Dennis had ever been anywhere near a farm. To them, it was a different world. But to Polly it was home.

She showed them Joan the goat. Joan stared at them. Daring them to come closer. Norman and Dennis decided not to take the chance. The pigs were safer. They were behind the pigsty wall. Polly leaned over to scratch the mother pig's back. But Norman and Dennis couldn't stand the smell.

"I suppose you don't have smells in the city," Polly mocked.

The hen-house was next on the list. Polly opened the door. Norman and Dennis were about to look inside when, suddenly, there was a crazy squawking and flapping of wings. A hen flew out.

Norman jumped back in surprise. The next thing, the two boys were sprawling on the ground. The hen landed on Dennis's chest. Polly grinned down at them.

That was it. Norman and Dennis had had enough. It was time to escape. They jumped to their feet and raced off across the farmyard. Polly just watched them go. She wasn't worried. They didn't even know where they were going. They'd have to come back to her in the end.

Norman and Dennis raced across a field, pretending

to be fighter planes. Then they dropped to the ground. It was their turn to grin.

"We showed her all right," said Dennis.

"Yes. We showed her," Norman agreed.

They stretched out on the grass and closed their eyes. The sun was beating down.

"Like being on holiday, isn't it?" said Norman.

"I don't know," said Dennis. "I've never been on holiday. What's it like?"

"It's like this," Norman told him.

It was like being on holiday. The countryside was fresh and peaceful.

Then a cow mooed! It wasn't a quiet, distant moo. It was a very loud, very close moo.

Norman opened his eyes. A cow was staring down at him. Norman sat up. There were other cows all around them. And more were on their way.

"Dennis!" said Norman. "We're surrounded."

Dennis sat up. He grabbed hold of Norman. The cows were inching closer all the time, their wet noses pushing forward and enormous tongues poking out.

"What are we going to do?" said Dennis.

Norman didn't know. He was afraid to move. He just sat there and hoped the cows would go away. But they didn't. They looked as though they were planning to stay all day.

Then they heard a voice. "What's the matter? Are you frightened of cows?"

It was Polly.

She clapped her hands and strode forward. The cows parted. As if by magic, a path opened through the middle of the herd.

Polly looked down at Norman and Dennis.

"Do you like it in the country then?" she asked.

Norman and Dennis said nothing. They just followed Polly back through the cows to safety. They'd learnt their lesson. Polly might be a girl but she knew what she was doing. And they needed her more than she needed them.

Polly led the way back to the farmyard. It was time to show the townies what life on a farm was all about. Norman watched while Polly and Dennis gave one of the calves a drink.

"What are you looking at?" Polly demanded.

"Do you want to be in our gang?" Norman asked.

Polly shook her head. "No!" she told him. "But you can be in mine."

If there was going to be a gang, Polly was going to be boss. After all, this was her territory. Norman and Dennis looked at each other and grinned. They'd settle for that.

A large, black car drove in off the road, sounding its hooter and scattering the hens. Polly led the way round to the yard. She had an idea who it was. She was right. It was Mr Grainger from Westbourne Hall. He was talking to Amy at the garden gate.

Polly, Norman and Dennis watched from behind
Grainger's car. Amy was counting money into his
outstretched hand.

"What's going on?" Dennis whispered.

"It's the rent," Polly hissed. "Grainger is our landlord."

Wells Farm was part of the Westbourne Hall estate. For the last couple of years, it had been owned by Grainger. He was not a good landlord.

"We hide behind the settee when our rent man comes," said Dennis.

Polly shushed him. Grainger was speaking.

"Bit of a struggle, isn't it?" he said. "Now your son's away?"

"Doing his duty," said Amy.

Polly's father had joined the army six months earlier. Since then, Amy had had to run the farm on her own. It wasn't easy.

"It's not right," Grainger insisted. "Old woman struggling to run a farm on her own."

Amy knew what Grainger was getting at. He wanted her off the farm. He'd said so before. But Amy was determined to stay.

"I told you, the only way I'm leaving here is for the graveyard," she said. "And that's that."

But Grainger wouldn't be put off. "I'd make it worth your while. Say three hundred pounds if you get out straight away."

Three hundred pounds was a lot of money. It was more money than the farm would make in two or three years. But Amy still wasn't interested.

"Mr Grainger – this is my home," she said. "I've lived here all my life. My father and his father were born here—"

"Sentimental rubbish!" Grainger had heard enough. "There's a war on. The country needs every last scrap of food it can grow. People like you are holding up the war effort."

"Don't talk to me about the war effort," Amy was angry now. "My boy is risking his life while others are sat at home making money hand over fist."

Grainger knew Amy was talking about him. He didn't like it. "You'll wish you hadn't said that, old woman," he snarled. "It's going to get worse round here. And when it does, I'll have you out on your ear without as much as a penny."

Grainger turned and stomped off towards his car. "Get away from there!" he yelled at the children. They ran.

Grainger drove off in a rage. One thing was certain – he was out to cause trouble.

"He can't turn you out. Not as long as you pay the rent," Dennis told Polly. "That's the law."

But that wasn't what was worrying Polly. "Running a farm is hard work," she said. "I don't know how long Gran can keep going on her own."

"But she's not on her own, is she?" said Norman. "There's us now, isn't there?"

Polly looked at Norman and Dennis. How much help would they be? They barely knew one end of a pig from the other. But perhaps they could learn.

"I don't mind helping," Dennis volunteered. "But I'm not milking a bull."

Polly sighed. "You milk cows not bulls, stupid!"

"What do you do with bulls then?"

"You don't need to know that."

That was one thing they would have to learn for themselves.

———————

Mary hadn't stopped all day. As soon as she finished one job, Miss Millington gave her another. It was as if nobody had cleaned Westbourne Hall for twenty years.

By nightfall, Mary was exhausted. She lay in bed and wondered how long she could go on like this. It would be hard but she wasn't going to be beaten. Especially not by Grainger and Millington.

In the dining room, Grainger was telling Millington about his visit to Wells Farm.

"Well, if the old fool won't go of her own accord, she'll just have to be persuaded," Millington replied.

Grainger smiled. "That's what I was thinking," he said. "I mean accidents do happen, don't they?"

Later that night, a pair of wire cutters snipped through one of the Wells Farm fences. One by one, the cows started to drift out on to the road.

It was the first "accident". It wouldn't be the last.

SPIES ALL AROUND

"Mrs Hobbs! You must come right away."

Mr Jenkins was hammering on the front door of Wells Farm. It was early morning. Polly, Norman and Dennis were still in bed.

"Quick, Mrs Hobbs! There's an emergency."

The door flew open.

"Mr Jenkins, whatever's wrong?" Amy was alarmed. "It's not the invasion, is it?"

"Worse than that," said Jenkins. "It's your cows. The fence is down. They're all along the road."

"My goodness, no!"

Already Jenkins was hurrying back down the path. Amy set off after him, then stopped.

"Polly!" she yelled through the open door. "Get those boys up now!"

The more help the better, Amy thought. Even Norman and Dennis would be some use.

The two boys were better than nothing. But only just. They stood in the backgound and flapped their arms. They still didn't trust those cows.

As the last of the animals was herded back into the field, there was a blast on a car hooter. Phillip Grainger was waiting to get past.

"Bit of trouble I see," he shouted out as he drove on. "Wouldn't happen if people looked after their fences properly."

Polly, Norman and Dennis watched Grainger's car disappear down the lane. The more they saw of that man, the more they disliked him.

"Take no notice," said Amy. "He's not worth it."

"That's right," Mr Jenkins agreed. "Now somebody fetch me a pair of pliers and I'll get this fence fixed for you. The rest of you can get your breakfasts."

When Polly got back with the pliers, Mr Jenkins was examining the broken ends of the wire fence. He looked puzzled. "I know it doesn't make sense," he said. "But it looks to me as if this has been cut."

Polly was amazed. If the wire had been cut, who could have done it? And why? As far as Polly was concerned, there was only one suspect – Phillip Grainger. Hadn't he said there was going to be trouble?

Mr Jenkins twisted the strands of fence together. "There!" he said. "That should do it for now, Polly."

But Polly wasn't listening. She was still thinking about the cut wires.

Jenkins handed over the pliers and climbed on to his bike. "Still plenty of letters to deliver," he said. "Don't forget tonight's meeting in the Village Hall."

Jenkins wobbled off along the road.

Polly didn't even notice him go. Her gaze was fixed on the distant Westbourne Hall. If only we could find out what's going on there, she thought.

———>=•=<———

At Westbourne Hall, Mary was washing up the breakfast things. One by one, she dried the knives and forks and dropped them into the cutlery drawer.

It was then that she noticed the wire cutters. Mary reached for them. But a hand grabbed her wrist. It was Miss Millington.

"I'll look after those," Millington snapped. "You just get on with your work."

"But I've finished the dishes," Mary told her.

Millington glared at Mary. "Then get this table scrubbed," she ordered. "It's filthy."

Mary filled a bucket with water and started to scrub the top of the kitchen table. She had almost finished when the front doorbell rang. Mary put down the scrubbing brush and sneaked into the hallway.

Miss Millington was at the door. "No, she's not here," Mary heard her say.

Mary peered round the corner. Mr Jenkins was standing in the doorway.

"Not here?" he questioned.

"No," Millington told him. "She went out for a walk

earlier on. She just loves getting out into the countryside.
She could be away for hours."

Mary gasped. They were talking about her. And
Millington was telling lies.

"I should see her," Mr Jenkins insisted quietly. "It is
required."

"Some other time." Millington tried to close the door.
But Jenkins held it open.

"There's a Civil Defence lecture," he said. "Seven o'clock in the Village Hall. Perhaps I'll see her there."

"Perhaps," said Millington. She slammed the door in Mr Jenkins' face.

———⟫•⟪———

"But why would Grainger cut the fence?" Norman asked.

Polly was milking one of the cows. "All part of his plan to drive us off the farm, isn't it?" she said. "And it won't be the last thing he does either."

Norman thought about it. If Polly was right, and Grainger really was out to cause trouble for Amy, then it was even more important for him and Dennis to help out around the farm.

"You can start by feeding the pigs," Polly told them.

The pigs! That was something that Norman and Dennis were not looking forward to. The smell of the pigsty made them feel ill. Then Dennis had a bright idea. At least, it seemed like a bright idea. They could wear their gas masks – then they wouldn't be able to smell anything.

They raced back to the house and pulled on their gas masks. Then went to feed the pigs.

There were two problems with gas masks. It was hard to breath. And almost impossible to see.

In the end, Norman and Dennis found the pigsty.

They even found the gate to get in. But once they were inside, they couldn't find the pigs. They had no need to worry. The pigs found them! As they rushed forward to get their food, the pigs crashed into Dennis. Dennis slipped and grabbed Norman. The next thing they knew, Dennis and Norman were lying in the mud.

Two of the pigs escaped into the farmyard. Dennis and Norman chased after them. Hens flew in all directions. One of the pigs ran into the duck pond and wouldn't come out.

"What am I going to do with you?" Amy sighed when she saw them.

"We wanted to help," said Norman.

Amy nodded. She knew they were trying. And they couldn't help being townies. It would take some time to learn country ways.

Amy gazed at Dennis's gas mask. The goat had eaten half of it and it was in tatters. "What Mr Jenkins will say if he sees that, I hate to think," she told Dennis. "Put it back in its box. And just hope that Jerry doesn't pick tonight to try and gas us all."

Dennis was in luck. There was no gas attack that night and Mr Jenkins never looked at his gas mask. He was too busy warning the villagers about the black market.

"Watch out for spivs," he told the audience in the Village Hall. "Trying to sell cigarettes. Or soap. Or nylon stockings."

The audience nodded. Since the war began, there were lots of shortages. Some things were strictly rationed. You could only buy small amounts. Other things were hardly ever in the shops. Yet, there always seemed to be somebody around who could get hold of what you wanted. If you were willing to pay extra.

"If anybody tries to sell you something like that, you report them to the police," Mr Jenkins continued. "This has got to be stamped out."

Norman wasn't very interested in the black market. He was gazing round the hall to see who was there.

He spotted Mary. She was sandwiched between Grainger and Millington. Millington was watching her like a hawk.

Norman nudged Polly and Dennis. They turned round and stared at Mary.

"Pay attention!" Amy hissed. She poked them with her finger.

They turned back to the front just as Mr Jenkins changed the subject.

"Now, something we all need to be on the look-out for," he told the audience. "Spies!"

Suddenly, Polly, Norman and Dennis were interested. Spies were exciting.

"They come parachuting down at night," Mr Jenkins announced. "So look out for parachutists, because spies are everywhere."

Polly, Norman and Dennis were amazed. They'd never realised there were so many spies. But Mr Jenkins seemed certain.

"They're all around us," he insisted. "The person next to you is a spy. Your mother's a spy. Your best friend's a spy. I'm a spy!"

The whole audience gasped in astonishment.

"At least, I might be," said Mr Jenkins. "That's why it's important never to say anything that could be of use to the enemy. Because 'Careless Talk Costs Lives'. Remember that."

Norman closed his eyes and thought hard. He was determined to remember it. When he opened his eyes again, Mr Jenkins was showing the audience some spy posters.

"Here are some typical disguises," he pointed out.

Polly, Norman and Dennis paid close attention. There was a man in a smart suit. A factory worker in a headscarf. A farmer. And finally, a strange picture of a pretty young woman. On one side, she wore a summer dress. On the other side, a German uniform.

"Any of these people could be spies," Mr Jenkins told them. "So keep a look-out."

He didn't need to say that twice. If there were spies around then Polly, Norman and Dennis were going to find them.

They started the search as soon as the meeting was over. People were standing around chatting outside the Village Hall.

"I bet most of these are spies," said Dennis.

"How can they be?" asked Polly. "They'd all be spying on each other."

"Well one of them must be a spy," said Dennis. "Mr Jenkins said there were spies everywhere."

Norman was watching out for Mary. Finally, he saw her leaving the hall with Grainger and Millington.

"Glad you were able to come," Mr Jenkins said to Grainger.

Grainger forced a smile. "Wouldn't have missed it for the world, Jenkins," he said. "Never realised you were such an expert on spies."

"I try to keep informed," Mr Jenkins told him.

"Think you'd recognise one if you met one?" Grainger sneered.

"I'd have my suspicions," Mr Jenkins replied.

"Suspicions aren't enough though. You need proof."

Grainger tried to lead Mary and Miss Millington away. But Mr Jenkins blocked the path.

"How's Mary settling in?" he asked.

"She's fine. As you can see," Millington snapped.

But Mr Jenkins wasn't giving up. "Everything as it should be, Mary?"

Millington gripped Mary's arm. "Mr Jenkins is speaking to you, Mary." There was something threatening about the way Millington spoke.

Her grip on Mary's arm grew even tighter.

"Yes, thank you," said Mary. "It's a bit like being at home."

"That's the way," Mr Jenkins smiled. Millington started to push her way through the crowd. But Grainger noticed Amy.

"Bit of a mishap last night, then?" he gloated. "Difficult when you're on your own, isn't it?"

Amy looked him straight in the eyes. "I'm not on my own any more," she told him. "I've got my evacuees to help now."

Grainger stared at Norman and Dennis. "Well, let's hope nothing happens to them then." His voice was full of menace. But before Amy could reply, he was pushing his way through the crowd towards his car.

------≫●≪------

Amy and the children walked back to Wells Farm across the fields. Dennis kept watch on the sky through his telescope. He was looking for parachutists.

"There! That's one up there!" he pointed.

Polly looked up. "That's a cloud," she scoffed.

"Looks like a parachute to me," Dennis insisted.

"Dennis," said Norman. "If it was a parachutist they'd wait until it was dark, wouldn't they?"

Dennis thought about it. It was a good point. But he was taking no chances. He turned his telescope back to the skies.

Polly was thinking about Mary. "She doesn't look very happy, does she?" she said to Norman.

"No," Norman agreed.

Mary hadn't looked at all happy. But that was hardly surprising. Living with Grainger couldn't be much fun. And Miss Millington didn't seem any better. Perhaps they should try and talk to Mary.

"I bet she could tell us things about Grainger, as well," Norman said. "If we could get to see her."

Polly nodded. "It's worth a try."

But how could they do it? Seeing Polly without Grainger and Millington finding out wasn't going to be easy. Not easy at all.

Norman's head was buzzing when he went to bed. Everything going round and round in his mind. "Spies are everywhere." That's what Mr Jenkins had said.

But if spies were everywhere, there must be a spy in the village. Who was it? Who was nasty enough to be a spy? Suddenly, it came to Norman. It was obvious. There was only one person it could be.

"Dennis!" he said. "I just thought who the spy is."

Dennis was still looking for parachutists through the window.

"Who?" he asked.

"Grainger!" Norman told him. "The spy is Grainger."

———➤●◄———

Mary was hungry. She was always hungry. She had been sent to bed without supper again.

Then she remembered the half bar of chocolate under her pillow. But when she lifted the pillow, the chocolate had melted and spread itself all over the sheet and pillowcase. It hadn't spoiled the pound note. But she couldn't eat that!

She would have to go to sleep hungry again. But she couldn't. All she could think about was chocolate.

Suddenly, there were footsteps outside the bedroom door. Mary closed her eyes and pretended to be asleep. The door opened. There was a moment's pause. And then the door closed again. Mary opened her eyes. What was going on?

In the hallway, Grainger was getting ready to go out into the night.

"Time I was going," he told Millington as she came down the stairs. "Don't want to miss the contact."

"Be careful," Millington replied. "If anybody sees you, they'll get suspicious."

Grainger stepped outside. "I won't be seen," he said. "There's nobody for miles. Except for that old biddy at Wells Farm." He nodded towards the stairs. "What about the girl?"

"Dead to the world," said Millington. "I just checked."

"In that case," Grainger smiled. "I've got nothing to worry about, have I?"

But Grainger did have something to worry about. Because, as he set off into the night, Mary was watching from her bedroom window.

TROUBLE
FOR MARY

"This is the last of the marmalade."

Millington was spreading marmalade thickly on her breakfast toast. Mary was pouring tea. Grainger pushed his cup towards her.

"I've got to go in and see old Hubbard this morning," he told Millington. "I'll pick some up then."

Millington looked surprised. "I thought he couldn't get any."

"He'll get some. Or he won't get what he wants from me, will he?" said Grainger.

His eyes were fixed on Mary. She was trying hard not to yawn.

"Late going to sleep?" Grainger asked.

Mary hesitated. She didn't want Grainger to know that she'd seen him go out into the night.

"No, sir," she said quietly.

"Didn't get woken up by anything? Things going bump in the night?"

Mary shook her head.

"Good!" said Grainger. "Wouldn't like to think of you lying awake at night. Not healthy. Understand?" His voice was cold and threatening.

Mary understood. There was something going on that Grainger and Millington didn't want her to know about. She was going to have to be very careful.

<hr>

"He is a spy. I'm certain of it." Norman told Dennis.

But Dennis wasn't so sure. "He doesn't look like any of those pictures on the posters," he pointed out. "And what about Millington?"

"She's definitely not a spy, she's not pretty enough," said Norman.

The woman spy on the poster had been very pretty. Nothing like Miss Millington. She was more like a witch.

"Norman! Dennis!" Amy's voice echoed across the farmyard. She was on her way to the village shop. "Behave!" she warned them. "No getting into mischief while I'm away."

"We won't," said Norman. "We'll just be helping out."

Amy sighed. "Well don't go helping too much, will you?" she pleaded. "I couldn't stand another day like yesterday."

<hr>

When Amy arrived at Mr Hubbard's shop, half the shelves were empty. The shortages were getting worse. Especially things which were brought in by sea. German submarines were attacking British ships, trying to stop supplies getting through.

There were notices all round the shop.

"No sugar till next week."

"Cigarettes out of stock."

"Don't ask for chocolate. We haven't got it."

"It doesn't get any better," Amy said to Mrs Calver while they were waiting to be served. Mrs Calver was a housewife who lived in the village.

Mrs Calver shook her head. "Marmalade. That's what my Eddie likes. Do you think I can get any?"

Amy knew she couldn't. She'd tried to get some herself. "They say it's all stolen and ends up on the black market," she told Mrs Calver.

"I tried a recipe for carrot marmalade. Two weeks sugar ration it took," said Mrs Calver. "My Eddie took one mouthful and threw the rest in the bin."

"What can I do for you, Mrs Calver?" asked the shop assistant, finally.

"Marmalade!" said Mrs Calver.

The shop assistant sighed. Mrs Calver always asked for marmalade. "Try next week," she suggested.

But Mrs Calver persisted. "You're sure there's none under the counter?" she demanded. "That's what they do, you know," she told Amy. "Put things on one side.

Then sell them overpriced to them who've got plenty of money."

Before Amy could agree, the door opened and Grainger stormed in.

"Is Hubbard in?" he barked. "I am expected."

The shop assistant opened a door leading to the back room. "Best go through, Mr Grainger," she said.

As Grainger pushed past, he noticed Amy. "Well, well, Mrs Hobbs," he sneered. "No more broken fences, I hope."

"Didn't know you were so concerned," said Amy.

"Oh, yes." Grainger didn't look at all concerned. "See, I hate to think what else might go wrong!"

The two women watched Grainger disappear into the back room.

"I bet he won't have any trouble getting marmalade," said Mrs Calver.

"Money!" said Amy.

"But where's it come from?" said Mrs Calver. "That's what I want to know."

———⇒◗◖⇐———

"Well, where's it come from?" Millington was holding up the pound note that she had found under Mary's pillow.

"My mother gave it to me," Mary told her.

"No, she didn't," Millington insisted. "You stole it from my purse. Admit it!"

Mary blinked away the tears that were welling up in her eyes. She wasn't going to let Millington see her cry.

"If it's not stolen, why was it hidden in your room?"

Mary took a deep breath. "It wasn't hidden. I put it there to keep it safe."

"Not much of a liar, are you?" Millington scoffed.

"I'm not a liar at all," Mary shouted. "And if you don't believe me, you can write to my parents!"

There was a silence. Millington seemed uncertain what to say. She didn't want Mary's parents causing trouble. They might get in touch with the authorities. Millington didn't want them snooping around Westbourne Hall.

She turned away. "Perhaps I jumped to the wrong conclusion," she said. "A pound is a lot of money for a little girl to have."

Millington reached up and took a vase from the mantelpiece above the fireplace. She popped the pound note inside and put the vase back. "Should be safe there, shouldn't it?" she smiled. "I mean, we wouldn't want you to lose it."

Polly, Norman and Dennis had given up on work and were playing hide-and-seek instead. It was Dennis's turn to seek.

"Coming – ready or not!" he shouted.

Dennis ran out out into the farmyard and looked around. Where were they hiding? The door to the cowshed was half open. Dennis smiled to himself. That's where they were.

Dennis stepped inside. The cowshed was dark. There were threatening shadows everywhere.

"You can come out now," he shouted. "I know you're in here."

But there was no reply. And nobody moved.

Dennis strained his ears. Was that somebody breathing? Suddenly, something creaked behind him. He twisted round. There was nobody there. Was this a trick?

"It's all right," he said. "You can come out. I give up."

But still nothing happened. If Polly and Norman were in there, they weren't letting on.

Dennis gulped. There was definitely something strange. He could sense it.

Something scrabbled across the floor.

That was the final straw. Dennis had had enough. He turned and ran for the door. As he got there, the door burst open. A mysterious stranger blocked the doorway. Dennis ran straight into him. A rough pair of hands grabbed hold of him.

"Let go!" Dennis shouted.

But no matter how much he struggled, the hands didn't let go. They gripped him even tighter, lifting him off the ground.

"Help!" yelled Dennis.

Norman and Polly hurtled out of their hiding place. They crashed into the attacker. All four fell to the ground in a shouting, battling, scuffling heap of arms and legs.

"Hey you! That's enough now. Just pack it in," a voice ordered.

Private Wilson, a British soldier, was looking down at them. He had his rifle at the ready. The scuffling stopped.

Polly, Norman and Dennis rolled away from the attacker and picked themselves up. The attacker was wearing a coat with a yellow circle painted on the back. The yellow circle showed that he was a prisoner of war.

"Good job you turned up," Polly said to Wilson. "He was trying to kill us."

"Are you all right?" Wilson asked.

"Just about," said Dennis, rubbing at a graze on his leg.

"Not you!" said Wilson. "Him!" He nodded towards the man, who was staggering to his feet.

The children couldn't believe their ears. The soldier seemed more bothered about the prisoner of war than them.

"You OK, Luigi?" Wilson asked.

The prisoner of war nodded. "OK! Yes." He offered his hand to Dennis. "Now friends?"

Dennis took a step backwards. He wasn't going to be grabbed again. Norman and Polly weren't going to risk it either. Not until they found out what was going on.

That was what Amy wanted to know. "What in the name of goodness is going on here?" Amy charged across the farmyard, weighed down with shopping bags.

"Who's he?"

The prisoner of war stepped forward and bowed politely. "Luigi Balzoni, Signora."

Amy ignored him and turned to Private Wilson. "Well?"

"He's an Italian P.O.W," said Wilson. "Here to help out on the farm."

"Here to murder us in our beds more like," snapped Amy.

Wilson shook his head. "Not him. He's Italian. Glad to be out of the war. He wouldn't harm a fly."

"He won't have the chance," Amy told him. "You can take him back where he's come from."

But Wilson had no intention of taking Luigi back. "Sorry, Missis," he said as he marched towards the road. "I can't do that. My orders are to drop him off and pick him up again at six o'clock. And that's what I'm doing."

Wilson disappeared out of the yard, leaving Amy glaring at the Italian.

Amy was taking no chances. "In!" she ordered the children. "Before he slits our throats."

Amy locked and bolted the door. Then set Dennis to keep watch on Luigi through the window while Norman and Polly helped with the dinner.

"I don't know what they can have been thinking of, sending one of those Italians here," Amy said as they sat down to eat.

"He doesn't look very dangerous to me," said Norman.

"Oh, doesn't he?" said Amy. "I suppose you'd have him in here eating our food, would you?"

Norman shrugged. "I might. He looked hungry."

Dennis was standing up, trying to see out the window.

"Sit down, Dennis," Amy told him.

But Dennis didn't sit down. He was stretching his neck to get a better view of the yard.

Amy was getting angry. "Dennis! Sit down!"

"But Aunty Amy—"

"Just sit down!"

"But he's gone!"

Gone! Everyone got up and peered out the window. Dennis was right. Luigi wasn't there.

"He's escaped!" Amy shouted. She picked up the rolling pin and set off towards the scullery door. "We've got to find him before he murders half the village."

It didn't take long to find Luigi. They saw him as soon as they got outside. He had taken off his coat and was busy cleaning out the pigsty.

He looked across at them and held his nose. "Pigs! Big smells, yes?" He pulled a face.

Dennis started to laugh. The next minute everybody was laughing. Even Amy. From then on, Luigi was like one of the family.

Mary was more like a slave than one of Millington's family. She had cleared away the dinner things and washed up. Now she was polishing the huge dining room table.

It was hard, back-breaking work. It hadn't been polished for years.

After a while, Mary stopped to rest. Her eyes strayed up to the vase above the fireplace. Mary was still angry about that. Millington had no right to take her money away from her.

The house was quiet. Millington was probably upstairs having an afternoon nap.

Mary hurried over to the fireplace and reached up for the vase. It was higher than it looked. At last, her fingers managed to slide the vase towards the edge of the mantelpiece.

"What do you think you're doing?"

Millington's voice took Mary completely by surprise. She was so shocked that the vase slipped from her grasp and smashed on the floor.

Mary dropped to her knees and started to pick up the pieces. Perhaps it could be glued together again. Then she realised. The pound note had gone. Somebody had taken it. Mary looked up accusingly at Millington.

But Millington was ready for her. "Get up to your room at once," she ordered. "And stay there."

It was time to make contact with Mary. Dennis had made friends with Luigi and stayed behind to help him. So it was just Polly and Norman who sneaked through the woods towards the back of Westbourne Hall.

Getting to see Mary, without Millington or Grainger catching them, wasn't going to be easy. They had to keep a close look-out and pick the right moment.

It was then that they found the greenhouse. It looked unused. As though nobody had been inside it for years. The windows were so dirty, and the plants so overgrown, that nobody could see in from outside. But from inside they could just see the back of the Hall.

It was the perfect hideout. They could watch for Mary from there with no danger of being seen by Millington or Grainger. Not only that, but once Mary knew about it, it would make the ideal secret meeting place.

But, that afternoon, there was no sign of Mary. So, after a couple of hours, Norman and Polly hurried back to Wells Farm to tell Dennis about the hideout.

Up in her bedroom, Mary had written a letter to her parents. If they knew how unhappy she was, perhaps they would take her home. It was worth a try. Even if her father did tell her not to be so silly.

Then the door to Mary's bedroom opened and Millington stepped in. She was carrying a tray with a hunk of bread and a glass of water on it. That was all Mary was getting to eat.

"I hope this has taught you a lesson," Millington snapped as she slammed the tray down. "I won't have disobedience in this house."

She sounded just like Mary's father.

"You'll be allowed down tomorrow," Millington continued. "You can catch up with your work then."

Millington was about to leave when Mary held out the letter.

"Excuse me, Miss Millington," she said politely. "I'd be grateful if Mr Grainger could post this letter to my parents. Just to let them know I'm all right."

"Very well."

Millington took the letter from Mary and left the room. On the stairs, she tore open the envelope and read through the letter. Then she put it on the fire. That was one letter that was never going near a postbox.

Chapter 5

THE POSTER COMES TO LIFE

"Aunty Amy! Come quick!"

Dennis ran across the farmyard shouting. Something was wrong.

An alarmed Amy appeared in the doorway. "Whatever's the matter with the boy?"

"It's the goat!" Dennis gasped.

"What about it?"

"The garden!"

Dennis turned and raced back the way he'd come, with Amy and Norman close behind.

The vegetable garden lay in tatters. Somehow, the goat had got loose in the night and had munched her way steadily through most of the plants.

"How did she get loose?" asked Norman.

"Accidents happen," sighed Amy.

"The rope must have broke," said Dennis.

Luigi shook his head. "Not break," he said. He was looking closely at the two ends. "Knife!"

Somebody had cut through the rope! But before

anyone could say anything else, Mr Jenkins arrived on his bike. He was waving an envelope.

"Letter for Master Norman Starkey!" he shouted out.

Norman gave a whoop of excitement. A letter! It had to be from his mother.

Norman was right. He read the letter through while Amy made Mr Jenkins a cup of tea.

There wasn't much news. She had moved into a one-bedroomed flat, not far from the munitions factory where she worked. It was only tiny but would do for the time being. There had been more bombing raids but she was safe and well. That was all. Apart from telling Norman to be good and not to get into trouble.

Suddenly, Norman felt very lonely. All he could think about was his mother and home. He didn't even hear what Mr Jenkins had to say when he heard that the goat's rope had been cut.

"Could be sabotage," Mr Jenkins suggested. "They say there are agents everywhere. Trying to ruin the war effort."

"Like spies, you mean?" asked Polly. Her eyes sparkled with excitement.

"Saboteurs! Spies! Same difference," Mr Jenkins told her. "Bad news."

Norman was still in a world of his own. He didn't even notice Luigi walk past the window. But Mr Jenkins did.

"Good job I managed to get you some help," he smiled at Amy.

"You, was it?" said Amy. So that was why Luigi had been sent to help. Mr Jenkins had organised it.

"Good worker, is he?" he asked.

"He'll do. Till my boy gets back from the army."

Jenkins finished his tea and picked up his cap. "Remember," he told Polly and Dennis. "Keep your eyes peeled for strangers. Anybody acting suspicious. That sort of thing."

"We are doing," said Polly.

Jenkins looked across at Norman. He hadn't said a single word since he'd opened his letter.

"Everything all right at home, Norman?" Jenkins asked.

Norman just stood up and walked outside.

Jenkins turned to Amy. "That wasn't like Norman. Something must be wrong."

Amy shook her head. "Just needs time on his own," she said.

Norman sat on the wall by the vegetable garden watching Luigi. Luigi was doing his best to save as many plants as he could.

"Polly's going to show me the hideout. Are you coming?" Dennis had come looking for Norman.

But Norman didn't want company. He got down off the wall. "You go," he told Dennis. "I'm going for a walk by the river."

Norman wandered off towards the road. Luigi watched him go. "He not good today?" he asked Dennis.

"I think he's missing home," said Dennis.

Luigi nodded. "Ah yes," he said. "Luigi also."

Because of the war, lots of people were missing home.

———>●<———

It was washday at Westbourne Hall. So Mary was working harder than ever. Water had to be heated and tipped into a tub. Then washing was put in and pounded up and down with a wooden paddle to get the dirt out. Finally, it was squeezed between the heavy rollers of a mangle to get rid of the water and hung on the line to dry. It would take all day. And already Mary felt worn out.

Still, there was one good thing about it. Being in the washhouse meant that Millington didn't keep poking her nose in all the time.

Mary lifted a sopping wet sheet up out of the water and fed it between the rollers. It wasn't easy.

"Want any help?" a voice called out from behind.

Mary looked round in alarm.

Polly and Dennis were standing in the doorway.

———>●<———

Norman sat by the river reading his letter for the tenth time. He didn't hear the footsteps behind him. A hand grasped his shoulder.

Norman twisted round. A soldier was towering above him. A soldier in the uniform of an American G.I.

Norman jumped to his feet.

"It's OK!" said the G.I. "Nothing to be afraid of. I'm Mike Johnson. I'm from the U.S. base a few miles down the road."

Norman just stared at him.

"Looking for the best place to fish," Mike explained. "Thought you might know."

Norman shook his head. His letter had dropped to the ground. Mike Johnson knelt down to pick it up.

"That's mine!" Norman held out his hand for the letter.

"Sure!" said Mike. He handed the letter to Norman. Then his hand went to his pocket and he pulled out a pack of gum. "You like gum?" he asked.

Dennis was helping with the washing. "They wouldn't starve me," he said as he turned the mangle's handle. "I'd pinch some food when they weren't looking."

Mary was telling Dennis and Polly how she was being treated by Miss Millington.

"And what about Grainger?" asked Polly. "What's he like?"

"Horrible!" said Mary.

"We think he's a spy," said Dennis.

"A spy?" Mary repeated.

"And we're going to catch him," Polly told her. "Do you want to help us?"

Mary nodded. She'd do anything at all to get her own back on Grainger and Millington. But how could they do it? Even meeting Polly, Dennis and Norman, without Grainger and Millington finding out, was going to be difficult.

"But we've got a hideout," said Dennis proudly.

Polly and Dennis told Mary about the greenhouse.

"We can meet there," said Polly. "Do you want to see it now?"

Mary thought for a moment. Leaving the washhouse was a risk. But if she was going to get her own back on Millington and Grainger, she was going to have to start taking risks.

"All right," she said. "But we'll have to be quick."

Mary ran to the door. Then turned back. There was a look of panic on her face.

"What is it?" said Polly.

"It's Millington," Mary whispered. "And she's coming this way."

＊＊＊

"Just loosen your wrists a little." Mike Johnson was teaching Norman to fish. Norman was staring across the river at the float bobbing in the water. Already the homesickness was forgotten.

"I guess it's not easy for any of us," Mike said. "Before this war, I was never more than twenty miles away from home. Now look at me."

There was a ripple of water near the float.

"Make the most of it. That's what my old man told me," Mike smiled. "And that's what I aim to do. Know what I mean?"

Norman nodded. He knew what Mike meant but he was concentrating too hard to speak. Suddenly, the float dipped down.

Mike jumped to his feet. "Hey!" he shouted. "I think we made a catch."

———

Millington stood in the doorway of the washhouse. "What's going on here then?" she snapped.

Mary looked round in alarm, as though Millington had taken her completely by surprise.

Millington stared at Mary. She thought she'd heard voices as she came across the yard but Mary was on her own. There was washing everywhere.

"This should be finished by now," Millington told her. "What have you been doing?"

Mary opened her mouth to speak but before she could say anything, Millington had turned on her heel. "Don't bother to explain," she said over her shoulder. "Just get on with it."

Millington's footsteps crossed the yard back to the house.

"All right now," Mary hissed.

The lid of one of the laundry baskets lifted and Polly and Dennis jumped out.

"That was close," said Polly.

"You'd better go," Mary told them.

"But what about the hideout?" asked Polly.

Mary wasn't worried about the hideout. She'd find it herself once she could get away. "It's all right," she told Polly. "Now please go before Millington comes back."

Mary checked outside and gave Polly and Dennis the all clear. They slipped out of the door and across the yard. A few minutes later, they were hurrying through the woods. They had almost reached the road when they came face to face with a young woman.

It was hard to say who was more surprised. They stared at each other in silence. Then the young woman spoke. "I was trying to get to the house," she said. "I saw it through the trees. I thought I might be able to get some help there. I'm hopelessly lost."

"Lost?" Polly repeated. There was something familiar about the woman. Polly felt that she had seen her somewhere.

"My bike is back on the road," the woman told them. "Perhaps you can help by pointing me in the right direction?"

Polly nodded. She was too excited to speak. She'd just remembered where she'd seen the woman.

"I think I've seen her before," Dennis said as the woman made her way back towards the road.

"You have," Polly agreed. "And so have I. It's the woman on the spy poster."

Dennis's mouth dropped open. Now he remembered. Polly was right. It was just as though the spy poster had come to life.

The young woman was climbing on to her bicycle. She had a small haversack on her back. Over one shoulder she had a camera and over the other was a pair of binoculars. Just the things that spies needed.

"These country lanes all look the same to me," the woman was saying. "It's like being in a foreign land. There aren't even any signposts around."

She was right. The signposts had been taken down to make it more difficult for the Germans if they invaded.

Polly nodded. "They've taken them away. To fool spies," she said.

"Well it certainly works," the woman replied. "Now perhaps you can tell me the way to Ombersleigh Childenham." She pronounced the name of a nearby village all wrong.

Polly corrected her. And gave the woman a series of directions.

"Thank you," the woman said. "That's very helpful."

She was eager to get going but Polly hadn't finished. "That's a nice camera," she said.

"It's a Leica," the woman replied. "I take a lot of photographs."

And she pedalled off down the lane. She needn't have hurried. Polly had sent her the wrong way. In ten minutes, she would be hopelessly lost again.

Polly and Dennis raced back to Wells Farm to tell Norman. An American forces jeep was parked in the farmyard.

"A jeep!" said Dennis. "What's a jeep doing here?"

They soon found out. Mike Johnson was walking down the path with Norman and Amy right behind him.

"Hey!" he called out. "You must be Polly and Dennis. Am I right? Norman told me all about you."

Polly and Dennis just stared.

"This is Lieutenant Johnson," Amy announced.

"Mike. Call me Mike."

Polly and Dennis were puzzled. What was the G.I. doing here? They looked to Norman for help. He just held up a tiny fish on the end of a line. "I caught a fish," he grinned.

"And before I go," said Mike. "I'm going to take a picture of it. And everybody else too."

Mike pulled a camera from his pocket and lined everyone up in front of the jeep. The shutter clicked. "I'll get this developed and bring you a copy over," he said.

Suddenly, Polly found her voice. "That's a nice camera," she told Mike.

Mike looked surprised. "Just a Kodak," he said. "Nothing much."

"Is a Leica a good camera?" Polly asked.

Mike smiled. "The best. But I wouldn't use one right now. It's German."

From that moment, any doubts about the woman in the woods being a spy disappeared from Polly's mind.

———>•<———

"I'd say a German camera settles it," she told Norman that night as they were doing the washing up.

"And there's the poster," added Dennis.

Polly nodded. "She looked just like it. Didn't she, Dennis?"

"Like two peas in a pod," Dennis agreed.

Norman thought about it. There certainly seemed to be plenty of evidence. Perhaps there were two spies – Grainger and the woman.

"Anyway, I sent her the wrong way," Polly said proudly. "She's probably still lost now."

There was a knock on the door. Polly hurried to answer it. Who could it be at this time of night?

Polly stepped back in shock.

The "spy-woman" was glaring in at her. "You!" she snarled. "I want to speak to you, madam!"

BOMBS IN THE COUNTRY

Polly backed across the scullery with the woman after her.

"You sent me in totally the wrong direction! Why? That's what I want to know."

Polly couldn't think what to say. But a second voice came to her rescue.

"And what I want to know is – who are you? And what are you doing in my house?"

Amy was standing at the kitchen door, looking like fury. Immediately, the woman calmed down.

"I'm sorry," she said. "My name is Vivienne Belling. And I've been riding round in circles for the last two hours. Thanks to this little madam here." She pointed at Polly.

Amy turned a suspicious gaze on her granddaughter. "Polly! What have you been up to now?" She didn't wait for a reply. Instead she said, "You better come in, Miss Belling. And I suppose you could do with a spot of supper as well."

For the first time, Vivienne Belling smiled. "Thanks. I'm absolutely starving," she said.

Polly was horrified. Her grandmother was asking a spy in for supper!

To Polly's disgust, Amy served Belling with thick buttered toast. And tea in her best china cups. She was treating her as an honoured guest. And it got worse.

"It's much too dark for you to be cycling into the village now," Amy said. "You'll just have to spend the night here."

"Oh no, I couldn't possibly," Belling replied.

But Amy insisted. "You can have Polly's bed," she said. "Polly can sleep down here."

And so Norman and Dennis were packed off upstairs. And Polly ended up on a camp bed in the corner of the kitchen. At first, Polly was livid. But then she realised that now she would be able to listen in to every word that Vivienne Belling said.

Amy and Belling sat in front of the fire and talked. About the war. About Polly's father going off to join the army and the way Amy was struggling to keep everything going. About the way Grainger was trying to get her off the farm. And about the "accidents" that were happening.

Belling seemed interested in Amy's story, but finally she steered the conversation round to the American base.

"It can't be far away," she suggested.

"Now, that I couldn't say for sure," Amy was being careful. "I reckon it's best not to know too much about such things."

Belling was surprised. "Really? Why's that?"

"What you don't know, you can't tell," said Amy. "After all, careless talk costs lives."

"But we can trust each other," Belling smiled. "Or do you think I might be a spy?"

"You might be," said Amy. "But there again, so might I."

The two women laughed at the idea. But to Polly it was further proof that Vivienne Belling really was a spy.

———⟫◆⟪———

Mary had been trying to sleep but it was no use. She was too hungry. She got out of bed and switched on the light. She opened the wardrobe door and checked her coat. Some time ago, she had found a shop which had boiled sweets. She bought a quarter and ate one every now and then as a treat. She pulled the bag out. All that was left was sweet papers.

If she wanted something to eat, she would have to steal it.

Mary slipped out of her bedroom and made her way downstairs. She could hear Grainger and Millington arguing in the dining room. They could go on like that for hours. All she needed was five minutes.

Moonlight was streaming in through the kitchen window. Mary's eyes went straight to the table. Her mouth started to water. A loaf of bread, a cold joint of meat, a huge slab of cheese and several jars of pickles had been left out. It was like a banquet.

Mary took the carving knife and cut herself a chunk of bread and cheese. She bit into it hungrily. This was going to be a real midnight feast. She was just dipping her hand into the pickle jar when she heard the door to the dining room open and the light in the corridor went on. Millington and Grainger were on their way.

Mary's eyes flicked round the room, desperately searching for somewhere to hide. In a panic, she dived under the kitchen table.

The door flew open and Grainger stormed in. The argument was still going on.

"I've told you before, I decide when it's safe," he snapped. "It's me that takes all the risks."

"What do you want? A medal?" Millington sneered. "All I'm saying is we're not doing enough. This war won't last for ever. Which do you want to be – a winner or a loser?"

"We'll come out on the right side," Grainger was looking for his torch. He was dressed to go out again. He started to move towards the door.

"What's the matter, Phillip?" Millington scoffed. "Losing your nerve?"

Grainger turned on Millington. "When I've got rid of that lot at Wells Farm, then we can think about stepping up operations."

But Millington wasn't giving up. "And how long do you think it'll be before those people at the base realise what's happening?" she asked.

Grainger had had enough. "Now's not the time," he said as he left the room.

Millington followed him outside. "You're late," she complained. "They'll think you're not going to turn up."

Grainger twisted round to answer her. But, as he did so, he noticed a light shining from Mary's bedroom. "Just a minute," he said. "That girl. What's she up to?"

He started back towards the house but Millington stopped him.

"Leave this to me," she said.

Millington stormed back into the house. Whatever Mary was up to, there was going to be trouble.

Millington rushed up the stairs and threw open the door to Mary's bedroom.

The light was still on. But Mary seemed to be fast asleep in bed. The noise of the door opening woke her. Still yawning, she looked across at Millington.

"Is it time to get up?" Mary asked sleepily.

"Your light is on!" Millington snapped.

"I must have fallen asleep reading," Mary yawned.

Millington was taken by surprise. She was lost for words. "Don't you know it's against the law to waste electricity?" she said finally. "There is a war on."

Millington flicked off the light and slammed the door behind her.

In the dark, Mary grinned. She took a huge chunk of cheese from under the bedclothes and bit into it. It had been close but it had been worth it. Not only had she managed to get some food, but she had fooled Millington as well. It was her first victory in the war between them. And it wasn't going to be the last.

<hr />

When Polly woke, Vivienne Belling had left.

"She's gone about her business," was all Amy would say when Polly asked where she'd gone.

"And what is her business?" Polly wanted to know.

"Taking photographs for the Government," said Amy. "To show what it's like living out here in the country while this wretched war is on."

And with that, Amy hurried outside to get on with her work.

"Photographs for the Government!" Polly snorted. "For Hitler, more like. That's what she's up to. Spying!"

But Polly, Norman and Dennis had not seen the last of Vivienne Belling. The woman was everywhere. And, wherever she went, she asked questions and took photographs. In the end, about the only person Belling hadn't been seen with was Grainger.

"If only we could catch the two of them together," said Polly.

"Perhaps Mary's seen them meeting up at the Hall," Norman suggested.

Polly nodded. "We'll go over and find out tomorrow."

Polly, Norman and Dennis were sitting in the barn behind some bales of straw. It was a good place to talk. Nobody else could hear them there.

Suddenly, Dennis looked up from his comic. He was reading a story about a spycatcher. And in the story it listed all the things that a spy needed.

Dennis read out the list. "A pair of binoculars. A camera. A book of secret codes. And a something else beginning with W."

Polly looked over his shoulder. "A wireless transmitter."

"That's it. A wireless transmitter," Dennis agreed. "What is a wireless transmitter?"

"Sends messages back to Germany," said Norman.

"Do you think Belling's got one of them then?" asked Dennis.

"Don't be stupid," Polly told him. "She only had a haversack."

"Grainger might have one though. It could be hidden in Westbourne Hall," Norman pointed out.

But that thought was forgotten as Mike Johnson's jeep turned into the farmyard.

Mike had two presents for them. A copy of the photograph that he'd taken. And a huge block of chocolate.

"Chocolate!" grinned Norman. "I can't wait."

"Oh yes, you can," Polly hissed as she grabbed the chocolate. "We're dividing this four ways. Next time we see Mary."

It was several days before they got to see Mary.

"I couldn't get away," she told them when she finally turned up at the greenhouse.

Carefully, Polly divided the chocolate into four parts. She gave the biggest share to Mary. She needed it most.

For a while, nobody spoke. The chocolate was too good. Then Polly remembered the question they wanted to ask Mary. Had she seen Vivienne Belling talking to Grainger?

Mary thought for a moment. "No. She could be meeting him at night though."

"At night?" said Polly.

"I've watched him," said Mary. "Grainger goes out to do something at night. And whatever it is they don't want anybody to know about it."

That was exactly what Polly, Norman and Dennis wanted to hear. Grainger was up to no good. But what was he doing?

On the way home, they found Luigi mending the gate to one of the fields. Almost immediately, Grainger drove up.

"What the devil do you think you're up to?" he demanded.

"Not doing nothing," said Polly.

"Not you!" Grainger snapped. "Him!" He was pointing at Luigi.

Luigi looked puzzled. "I fix the gate for Mrs Amy," he shrugged.

"He's working for us now," said Polly proudly.

Grainger looked as though he were about to explode. "Oh yes?" he snarled. "Well, we'll have to see about that, won't we?"

With a screech of tyres, the car pulled away.

"What is it with him?" Luigi was bewildered. "He sleep bad or something?"

Norman knew it was more than that. Grainger was out to cause even more trouble for Amy. But when they got back to Wells Farm, Amy was too bothered about dinner to listen. She sent Norman to collect eggs while Polly and Dennis went to look for mushrooms in the top field.

Norman was on his way back when he heard the plane. It was a sound that he knew only too well. He looked up in alarm, searching the sky for the tell-tale outline.

"What's wrong?" asked Amy. She could see the worried look on Norman's face.

"That plane!" said Norman.

That was all Amy needed to hear. The tone of Norman's voice said everything.

"Oh my Good Lord," Amy cried out. "Polly and Dennis!"

Dennis was kneeling down picking a mushroom.

"Not that!" Polly told him. "That's a toadstool. Don't you know the difference?"

But Dennis wasn't listening. His ears had picked up another sound. The sound of a plane coming their way.

Polly heard it as well. She wasn't worried. "It's all right," she said. "It's one of ours."

But Dennis knew better. "Don't you know the difference?" he asked. "That's a German plane." He grabbed hold of Polly and started dragging her across the field. "Come on!" he shouted. "Run!"

Dennis and Polly raced like mad towards the farm. But there was no way they could outrun an aeroplane. Suddenly, it was right above them. The noise was deafening. And then came a second sound. The whine of bombs.

"Get down!" Dennis screamed.

He pushed Polly to the ground and threw himself down beside her.

The next moment the bombs exploded in a huge cloud of dust and smoke. Then there was silence.

Chapter 7

SURPRISE

Everything was still. The dust settled. The smoke cleared. But still nothing moved. Then Dennis lifted his head. Polly lay next to him face down.

Dennis grabbed Polly's shoulder. "Polly!" He shook her. "Polly! Wake up!"

But Polly didn't move.

Dennis rolled her on to her back. Her eyes were tight shut. He shook her again. "Wake up, Polly! Please wake up!"

Suddenly, Polly's eyes flicked open. "You were right," she said. "It was one of theirs."

"You've had a lucky escape," Doctor Simpson took off his stethoscope and dropped it into his bag. "No lasting damage. Ringing in the ears, perhaps. Best stay in bed today."

Polly and Dennis were sitting side by side in bed. They were still shocked, but pleased to be the centre of attention.

"Any news of the plane?" Doctor Simpson asked Mr Jenkins.

"It crash landed. Pilot was just unloading his bombs. Doubt if he even saw the children. No sign of him yet. Got the army out looking."

"Bad business," said the doctor. He wrote out a note for some medicine. "Nothing too nasty," he told Polly and Dennis.

"Don't believe him," whispered Norman. "It'll be horrible."

Norman went straight off to the village to fetch the medicine. He was taking a short cut through the churchyard when he saw them. Grainger and Belling! Deep in conversation.

Norman ducked behind a gravestone. This was just what he had been hoping to see. He crawled forward. But before he could get near enough to hear what the two were saying, they walked away.

Keeping under cover, Norman followed them towards the church gate. Beyond, Norman could see Grainger's car.

Grainger opened the car door and reached inside. He pulled out a small, brown paper package. He checked that nobody was watching. Then he handed the parcel to Vivienne Belling. Immediately, she slipped it into her bag and hurried away.

That was enough for Norman. He couldn't wait to tell Polly and Dennis about it!

"What do you think was in the packet then?" Polly asked.

"Could have been chocolates," Dennis suggested.

Polly snorted. "Don't be stupid! What would spies be giving each other chocolates for?"

It didn't seem stupid to Dennis. "There could be secrets hidden inside them. That way, if they're caught, they just eat the evidence."

Norman sighed. Sometimes Dennis's imagination ran away with him. "It doesn't matter what it was," Norman pointed out. "They know each other. That's the proof we were looking for."

"Now all we need is to find Grainger's wireless transmitter," Polly agreed.

She was right. If they could find that, then nobody would doubt that Grainger and Belling were spies.

"That's a job for Mary," said Norman. "I'll go and see her now."

Mary was outside cleaning windows. Westbourne Hall had dozens of windows. And Mary had been cleaning them all day. There were still plenty left to do.

"Mary! Over here!"

Mary looked round. There was no one there. Then Norman's head popped up from behind the dustbins.

Mary carried on with her work. Grainger or Millington might be watching. "You shouldn't come here," she told Norman.

"I had to," Norman hissed. "It's important. We've got to find Grainger's wireless. For sending messages. It must be hidden somewhere inside the house."

Before Mary could reply, the kitchen door opened and Millington stepped out.

Norman ducked down behind the bins. Mary carried on as though nothing was wrong.

Millington glared at Mary. "Is that all you've done?" she snapped.

Mary said nothing.

"You'd better come in and get on with the evening meal," Millington told her. "You'll have to finish the windows tomorrow."

Millington slammed the door.

As soon as she'd gone, Mary turned to Norman. "I'll try and look," she said. "But it won't be easy. When they're not here, they lock me out."

Norman just smiled. "You can do it," he said. "I know you can."

———⟫●⟪———

Norman was down early the next morning. Amy was still building up the kitchen fire.

Norman checked all round. "Any post, Aunty Amy?" he asked.

Amy looked puzzled. "Post? Not yet. Are you expecting something?"

Norman frowned. "No!" he said.

The next moment, there was a knock on the door.

"Perhaps that's Mr Jenkins now," said Amy as she hurried to open it.

It was Mr Jenkins. His voice boomed through the open door. "Special parcel for young Norman, Mrs Hobbs."

"My goodness!" said Amy. "You'd better come in."

But it wasn't Mr Jenkins who stepped into the room. It was a young woman.

Amy had never seen her before. But she guessed who it was.

Norman stared open-mouthed. Then he spoke a single word. "Mam!"

Mrs Starkey held out her arms. "Happy Birthday, Norman!" she smiled.

Norman raced across the kitchen and hugged her.

Amy knew just what to do. She put on the kettle. A cup of tea would work wonders.

Several cups of tea later, everyone was gathered round the table which was cluttered with wrapping-paper and presents. A rubber ball, a home-made balaclava, some crayons, and a wooden plane.

"War or no war, I couldn't miss his birthday," Mrs Starkey was telling Amy. "They said I could have today off as long as I worked extra next week."

Amy poured another cup of tea.

"Anyway," Mrs Starkey carried on. "I got as far as Bidwell Edge last night, then the rest of the way this morning."

Mr Jenkins had brought her out from the village in his car. It was just as well. She could never have walked it with all those presents to carry.

"Now there's one more thing," said Mrs Starkey. She placed the biggest parcel yet on the table. "I'm going to open this," she told Norman. "You put your fingers in your ears and shut your eyes."

Norman did as he was told while Mrs Starkey opened the final present. When he opened his eyes again, he saw a huge decorated birthday cake with burning candles.

Everyone sang "Happy Birthday" and Norman blew out the candles with one breath. Everybody clapped and cheered.

"Now," said Amy, picking up the bread knife. "Who's having first piece?"

Amy plunged the knife into the middle of the cake. There was a gasp of horror from Mrs Starkey.

The centre of the cake had collapsed. There was nothing inside it. It was made of cardboard.

Mrs Starkey was almost in tears. "It's an old hat box," she explained. "Decorated to look like a cake. It was the best I could do," she sniffed. "You just can't get the ingredients any more. The candles are real!"

Norman patted his mother's arm. "It's all right, Mam," he said. "It is. It's all right."

Amy jumped to her feet and pushed Norman, Polly and Dennis out of the kitchen. "You three get out of my way," she told them. "And I'll make a birthday cake."

Mike Johnson's jeep was just pulling up as the three children tumbled outside.

"Guess what, Mike?" Polly shouted out. "It's Norman's birthday."

"And his mum's come to see him," Dennis added.

"Well, that's quite a present," Mike grinned. "Happy Birthday, Norman."

Mike was pleased it was Norman's birthday. But he felt bad about not bringing him a gift. Then he remembered. He kept an old baseball glove in the back of the jeep. Perhaps that would do. He reached down and pulled it out.

"How about this as a present from me?" he asked.

Norman's face lit up. This was turning into a birthday to remember. He grabbed the glove.

"It's great," he told Mike, "What is it?"

———— >●€— ————

Mary was cleaning her fifth window of the day.

"You'll never make a window cleaner," Millington snapped. "This side's filthy." She locked the back door.

Grainger was getting impatient. It looked as if the two of them were going into the village.

"Make sure they're all finished by the time we get back," Millington ordered.

A couple of minutes later, the car disappeared down the drive and Mary was left on her own. Now was her chance to look for the wireless transmitter.

She quickly swilled over the rest of the windows. Then slid open the one that she had unlocked earlier. She climbed into the house. Grainger's bedroom was upstairs at the front. That would be the first place to look.

Mary hurried upstairs.

Grainger's bedroom was dark and spooky. A large desk was covered with papers. The huge bed was unmade. On the shelves were cases of stuffed animals. The room wasn't going to be easy to search.

Mary began with the wardrobe. Then she searched through a cupboard and a bedside cabinet before turning to a large chest of drawers. She started at the top and worked her way down. By the time she got to the bottom drawer, she was beginning to despair. There was no sign of a wireless transmitter nor anything else to suggest that Grainger was a spy. And she was running out of places to look.

It was then that she spotted the suitcase beneath the bed. Mary reached under and slid it out. She was sure this was going to be the place where the wireless was hidden. But when she opened it, her heart sank.

The case was stuffed full with bars of soap, bottles of perfume, packs of nylon stockings and packets of cigarettes. It was then that Mary heard the sound of Grainger's car coming up the drive.

"Oh no!" she gasped. "They're back!"

The car skidded to a halt at the front of the Hall. Millington jumped out. There was no sign of Mary.

"Get the shopping," she shouted to Grainger. "I'll look for the girl!"

She ran up the front steps and unlocked the door. "Mary!" she shouted as she stepped into the hallway.

There was no reply. She listened for a moment but the house was silent.

Millington hurried through to the back of the house and unlocked the door into the yard. She almost fell over Mary who was sitting on the step waiting to be let in.

Mary looked up and smiled sweetly.

———⇒●⇐———

"That surely was a fine piece of cake," Mike Johnson licked his lips. He was sitting on the front of his jeep watching Polly, Norman and Dennis take turns to use the baseball glove. Mrs Starkey was sitting next to him.

"Lucky you turned up when you did," she said.

Mike shrugged. "Came over this way to check up on a report about that German pilot."

Amy was leaning against the gate. "Have they not caught him yet?" She sounded alarmed.

"Nothing to worry about, Mam," said Mike. "He's probably miles away by now."

Mrs Starkey stood up. It was time for her to leave. She had a long journey in front of her, even though Mike Johnson had offered her a lift to the village.

Mike took something from inside the jeep and offered it to Norman's mother. "You deserve a present too," he said.

The smile disappeared from Mrs Starkey's face. "Nylon stockings!" she said. "Where are these from?"

Mike knew what was worrying her. "They're not black market," he said. "Though there's a heck of a lot of that stuff around, I know. We're even losing things off the base. But these are OK. From our P.X. shop."

Mrs Starkey smiled. "In that case, thanks," she said and popped the stockings in her bag. "Now I really must go."

Amy, Polly and Dennis waved goodbye as the jeep pulled away. But Norman was too upset to watch. As the jeep turned on to the road, he raced back to the farmhouse and went straight to his bedroom. Half an hour later, he was asleep. It was the only way he could ease the pain.

———⟫●⟪———

By the next afternoon, Norman felt better again. He had saved a piece of birthday cake to give to Mary. So Norman, Polly and Dennis set off for Westbourne Hall.

As they reached the hideout, Polly noticed that the door was slightly open. "I think Mary's already here," she said.

"Last one in is a Nazi," yelled Dennis.

The three of them dived for the door and scrambled in. Inside they stopped dead.

Lying propped up in front of them was the German pilot. A Luger pistol in his hand. It was pointing straight at them.

Chapter 8

THE PILOT

The pilot spoke. None of them understood German.
But the gun said everything.

A second voice spoke. "Just stay still!" Mary was
sitting on the floor not far away.

"How long have you been here?" Norman asked.

"A few minutes."

The pilot was slumped over to one side. With a groan of pain, he tried to straighten himself up.

"He's hurt," Mary told them. "Badly hurt."

The pilot grunted something else at them.

"What's he say?" gulped Dennis.

"I don't know," Polly answered. "But whatever it is – do it."

The pilot signalled them to sit next to Mary. Slowly, they edged their way across and slid to the floor. The gun never left them for a moment.

The pilot's uniform was heavily bloodstained. And his left arm was broken. His face was pale and drawn. He looked as though he was about to pass out.

Again he struggled to sit up. He propped his right arm on his left knee so that his Luger was pointing at the children.

The gun seemed to fill the greenhouse. They couldn't take their eyes off it. For a while, time stood still. They might have been there for two minutes or two hours.

Then the end of the gun started to drop down. The pilot was drifting into unconsciousness.

Slowly, Mary started to inch forward. Polly tried to stop her but Mary was determined to carry on.

Silently she edged towards the gun. Finally, she was within arm's length. She reached out to grab the drooping barrel. Suddenly, it flicked back into position.

The pilot was awake again. Eyes wide open. Staring at Mary. The gun pointing straight at her. For a moment, he seemed uncertain what to do. But then he realised he was in a hopeless situation. He'd gone as far as he could go. And anyway, he had no wish to harm the children. He loosened his grip on the gun and let Mary take it from him.

As Mary eased the gun out of his hand, he slumped sideways in a faint.

"Water!" Mary ordered. "Get him water!"

Polly found an old jam jar and ran to a stream in the woods to get water for the pilot.

Between them, they managed to sit him up and get him to take a few sips. Slowly, his eyes opened and he muttered his thanks.

"He must be hungry," said Mary. "Got anything to eat?"

"Only this," Norman showed Mary the birthday cake that he had saved for her.

"He'd better have it," said Mary.

Bit by bit, they fed the cake to the pilot. He was very hot. His temperature was sky high. Mary poured cold water on to her handkerchief and wiped his face.

"He needs a doctor," Mary told them.

They knew that what Mary said was true. But there was a problem. If they fetched a doctor to the pilot, then Grainger would find out that they had been in the greenhouse. Worse than that, he would realise that Mary had been meeting with the others. Then she would be in real trouble.

"You'd better go," Norman told Mary. "Then Grainger needn't know you've been here."

"All right," said Mary. "But please hurry."

"I'll go down to the telephone box by the bridge," said Polly. "I can telephone Doctor Simpson from there."

Mary and Polly left Norman and Dennis looking after the pilot.

"See if he wants more water," said Dennis.

Norman put the jam jar to the pilot's lips and he took another drink.

He smiled weakly and spoke a few words. Then he tried to push himself forward.

"Just stay still!" Norman told him. "There'll be help here soon."

But the pilot was feeling behind him. Trying to get hold of something with his good arm. Norman reached behind and pulled out a small waterproof wallet.

The pilot nodded his thanks. He took out some photographs and a letter and gave them to Norman. He indicated his uniform pocket. Norman slipped them into the pocket. Then the pilot gave the wallet to Norman.

"He wants us to have it," said Dennis.

Inside the wallet there were papers that were something to do with his flight plans. The boys leafed through them. They weren't certain what they were. But Norman was sure of one thing. If anybody found out about them, they'd be taken away.

"Hide them!" said Dennis.

There was an old biscuit tin in a pile of rubbish. Norman pulled it out. "This'll do," he said.

They put the papers inside. Replaced the lid. And pushed it back among the rubbish.

"We'll come back for them later," said Norman. "When there's nobody around."

Behind them, the pilot groaned and slumped to one side. Norman and Dennis rushed to help him. But just then the greenhouse door crashed open. It was Grainger. He had a shotgun. It was pointing at the pilot.

"Don't shoot him!" shouted Norman.

"What makes you think it's him I'm going to shoot?" Grainger snarled. He looked as though he meant it. But the next moment Polly burst in.

"Doctor Simpson's gone into Wenham," she gasped. "So Miss Millington telephoned Mr Jenkins. He's on his way."

Norman and Dennis stared open-mouthed. Why had Polly brought Grainger of all people?

———————◆———————

"What did you have to go and get Grainger for?" Norman demanded later.

"I didn't mean to, stupid," said Polly. "I was trying to get a lift to the telephone box and he came along."

The pilot had been carried from the greenhouse to the front of Westbourne Hall. Now he was being loaded into the back of Jenkins' car.

A crowd had gathered. Everybody was keen to see a real live German pilot. Mr Jenkins had brought the village policeman and Vivienne Belling out with him.

She was taking photographs as two of the farmworkers lifted the pilot on to the back seat of Jenkins' car. As they did so, one of the men knocked against the German's broken arm. He shouted out in agony.

"Watch out for his arm," Belling told them. "He says it's broken." Leaning into the car, Belling said something to the pilot. She spoke in fluent German.

"Did you hear that?" whispered Polly. "That proves she's a spy."

Jenkins and the policeman climbed into the car and set off for the hospital. The crowd started to drift away. It was all over. But Vivienne Belling wandered across to speak to Grainger.

"I bullied Mr Jenkins into bringing me out here," she said. "Now I'm stuck. I don't suppose you could run me back?"

Grainger smiled. "Yes, of course, Miss Belling. I've got one or two things to do first. Just come in for a minute."

Grainger started to lead Belling inside, then he remembered Polly, Norman and Dennis.

"I'm warning you three. If I catch you on my land again, I'll be pointing my shotgun at you for real. Now get out of here."

Polly, Norman and Dennis didn't need telling twice. They raced back to Wells Farm. As they ran into the farmyard, they met Luigi.

"Hey! You late! Signora Amy – she look for you. When she find you—" Luigi pretended to pass a knife across his throat. His meaning was clear. Amy was on the warpath.

A moment later, Amy appeared in the doorway. "And where have you three been until this time?" she demanded.

"Whatever you do – don't mention the guns," Polly whispered to the others.

"In!" said Amy.

Norman, Polly and Dennis trooped into the house.

Amy lined them up in front of her. She listened with growing horror to their tale of the German pilot.

"Goodness me," she said at the end. "You might all have been murdered. What would have happened if he'd had a gun?"

"He did have!" said Dennis.

Polly and Norman looked daggers at him.

"What?" said Amy.

Dennis tried to think of a way out of the mess he was in. "He did have . . . a broken arm!" he told Amy. "So he wouldn't have been able to use a gun, would he?"

Amy stared at Dennis. Her gaze was full of suspicion. But before she could question him anymore, there was a knock on the door.

Private Wilson was there with Luigi just behind him. Luigi didn't look happy.

"What's wrong with him?" Amy asked.

"He won't be coming tomorrow," said Wilson. "He's being moved to another farm."

"Moved?" Amy was shocked. "What's the matter?" she questioned Luigi. "Don't you like it here?"

Luigi was upset. "No, I want to come. Please!" he begged Wilson.

"Sorry," said Wilson. "It's nothing to do with me. They say they're sent where they're most needed," he told Amy. "But just between you and me, I think somebody's been pulling strings. He's being sent to Westbourne Hall."

Westbourne Hall! So Grainger had used his influence to get Luigi moved. To make life more difficult for Amy.

Wilson walked away but Luigi remained. "You very kind, Mrs Amy," he said. "This for my thanks."

He handed Amy a wooden crucifix that he had carved himself.

There were tears in Amy's eyes. "Thank you," she told him. "I hope one day you go back to your home in Italy."

Sadly, Luigi walked away.

Desperately, Amy blinked back the tears. "I won't let Grainger beat me," she said. "We managed before. And we'll manage again."

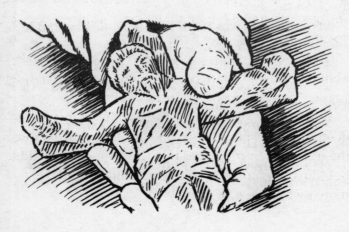

But in spite of Amy's determination, Polly, Norman and Dennis knew that Grainger was winning. Something had to be done soon if he was to be stopped.

"We could go to the police," said Polly as they moved the cows into a new field.

"He's got plenty of money and lives in a big house. Who's going to believe us when we tell them he's a spy?" said Norman.

Polly knew that what Norman said was true. "We need to catch them red-handed then," she said. "Him and Vivienne Belling. Then they'll have to believe us."

But that seemed like an impossible task. For the first time, they had doubts about whether they would ever be able to stop Grainger.

———⟫●⟪———

At Westbourne Hall though, Mary had no such doubts. She was determined to find out what Grainger was up to when he went out after dark.

From her bedroom, she watched as Grainger and Millington stepped out into the night. They spoke a few words. Then walked off in different directions.

Mary slipped downstairs and out through the front door. In the distance, Grainger was disappearing into the trees. She hurried after him. It was foggy and dark but Mary was going to stay on Grainger's trail. No matter what the risk.

THE SECRET QUARRY

Mary followed Grainger through the woods until he stopped at a place where a narrow track led off the lane. He signalled with his torch. Headlamps flashed back at him. The headlamps started to move down the lane towards Grainger.

Grainger walked down the track. As the headlamps got nearer, Mary could see that it was a lorry. The lorry turned on to the track and slowly followed Grainger out of sight.

Mary decided it was time to get back to Westbourne Hall. She would have to wait to find out where the track led.

———————>◦◦<———————

The next day, Polly, Norman and Dennis made their way through the woods towards the Westbourne Hall hideout. They were after the pilot's papers. But as they got near, they heard a loud hammering. They were in for a shock.

It was Luigi. He had almost finished boarding up the entrance to the greenhouse.

"Luigi!" Dennis yelled.

The Italian stopped hammering and turned in surprise. A broad smile spread across his face. "Hey! What you do here, huh?" he grinned.

"Not what are we doing?" said Norman. "What are you doing?"

Luigi pulled a face. "This Grainger – he say stop up the door so nobody get in."

Dennis ran forward. "But we've got to get in, Luigi. We left something in there."

Luigi shook his head. "No. See, all stopped up. Too late. Now please, you go. Grainger come back. Big trouble for you."

Suddenly, Mary appeared down the side of the greenhouse. "He's right. Grainger's on his way now," she said. "Come with me. I've got something to show you."

Mary led the way to the track that the lorry had driven along. On the way, she told them about what she'd seen the night before. Then about the things she'd found in Grainger's bedroom.

"So there was definitely no wireless transmitter," Norman couldn't hide his disappointment.

"Just the cigarettes and things," Mary told him.

"The wireless could be hidden somewhere else though," Dennis pointed out.

"Never mind that now," said Polly. "Look at this."

The track had come to a stop at an old quarry. Barbed wire was stretched across the entrance. And signs read – "DANGER – KEEP OUT" and "NO ENTRY!"

"I think they want to keep us out," grinned Dennis.

"Too bad," said Norman. He ducked under the wire. "We're going in."

There were tyremarks and footprints all over the floor of the quarry.

"That proves somebody's been here," said Norman.

But Dennis had found something much more interesting. In one corner of the quarry, a tunnel led up into the rock.

"Got the torch?" asked Norman.

Dennis reached into his pocket and pulled it out.

Norman turned to Polly and Mary. "You two keep a look-out," he told them. "Anybody comes – whistle."

"I can't whistle!" said Polly.

"I can!" said Mary. She pushed her fingers in her mouth and gave an ear-splitting blast. "My father says it's common," she grinned. "That's why I do it."

Norman and Dennis looked into the tunnel. It was very dark. Dennis passed the torch to Norman. "You go first," he said.

After a couple of minutes, they were in almost total darkness. There was no light in front or behind. Just the weak beam of the torch.

They stumbled on uphill for what seemed like miles.

They were getting nowhere. Then suddenly, without warning, the tunnel opened out and they found themselves in a brick-lined cellar.

Norman looked round. In one corner there were piles of boxes.

"Where are we?" hissed Dennis.

Norman was mystified. But then he realised. "Dennis!" he said. "You know where I think we are? Under Westbourne Hall!"

Dennis's eyes grew wide with fright. "Oh no!" he gasped. "What if Grainger catches us?"

They had to get away as quickly as possible. But the torch battery was getting low and neither of them wanted to go back through the tunnel without that. Then Norman spotted slivers of daylight. There was a door.

"This way!" he told Dennis. They were in luck. The key was in the lock. Norman turned it and opened the door. Light flooded in.

They were at the bottom of a flight of stairs leading up to ground level. Dennis closed the door while Norman checked that there was nobody around.

"All right," he called back down to Dennis.

But Norman had spoken too soon.

Grainger's voice echoed across the yard. "Get away from those steps!" He was striding towards them. He had a heavy walking stick in his hand.

He stopped at the top of the flight of steps. Looking down at them. "I thought I told you to stay off my land," he barked. There was a look of pure hatred on his face. "I think it's about time I taught you two a lesson!"

He raised his stick in the air ready to strike down at Norman and Dennis. But before he could do it, someone grabbed his wrist. It was Luigi.

Grainger was taken completely by surprise. He was even more shocked when Luigi twisted the stick out of his grip.

"What do you think you're up to, Balzoni?" Grainger gasped.

Luigi said nothing. Just broke the stick across his thigh and threw the two halves to the ground. "You go now. Please," he told Dennis and Norman.

The two boys inched past Grainger.

"You're going to wish you hadn't done this, you know," Grainger said, glaring at Luigi. Then he turned to Norman and Dennis. "And you two!" he snapped. "Get out of here now!"

Norman and Dennis raced through the woods back to Polly and Mary.

The two girls listened in amazement to the news about the tunnel and the escape from Grainger.

"We've just got to find out what's going on down here," said Norman, finally.

Mary nodded. "Next time there's a lorry," she said. "I'll follow it and see what they do."

It was a good idea. But very dangerous.

"You can't do it on your own," Norman insisted.

"No," Polly agreed. "Come for us first. Throw dirt at the bedroom window."

"All right," Mary smiled. "Now I'd better go. I've been away too long." Mary had never looked happier. "This is getting exciting, isn't it?" she said as she hurried away.

But a strange thing was happening. As Mary was getting more and more confident, Norman was starting to worry.

What Dennis said later made him worry even more. "They could be taking lorry loads of guns down there," he suggested as they sat in the barn. "Building up supplies. For parachutists."

"Guns?" said Polly. "You think so?"

"Or explosives!"

Norman knew then that they were getting out of their depth. If this was to do with guns and explosives, then they had to tell somebody.

"But who?" said Dennis. "Nobody'd believe us."

"Somebody might," said Norman. There was only one person who they could trust to listen to their suspicions – Mike Johnson.

⟶➤◄⟵

Mike listened carefully as they told him all about Grainger and Belling and the lorries in the night. At the end, he gave a low whistle.

"You know," he admitted. "This is all pretty hard to believe. I mean, Mr Grainger is like the big man round here. You got to have proof before you go grabbing hold of a guy like that and accusing him of being a spy."

"But we've got proof!" Polly insisted.

"Not that he's a spy," Mike pointed out. "Sure sounds like he's up to something. But I don't know what."

Norman's heart sank. "You're not going to do anything then?"

"Hold on!" Mike told him. "Did I say that? Maybe we can't touch Grainger yet. But Vivienne Belling is different. She's a stranger round here. Asking questions. Taking photographs."

"Speaking German!" Polly added.

Mike nodded. "I'd say that lady has one or two questions to answer. And if she ties in with Grainger, we'll have him as well."

Polly, Norman and Dennis gave a shout of excitement.

But Mike stopped them. "Now you guys listen," he warned. From now on, leave this to me. Don't do anything else till I get back to you. Promise?"

They promised. But it was a promise that was hard to keep. Especially a couple of days later when Mr Jenkins pedalled madly into the yard with the latest news.

"The police have got Luigi," he told Amy.

"Luigi?" Amy couldn't believe her ears. "Whatever for?"

"Stealing!" Jenkins told her. "Mr Grainger says he's been stealing from Westbourne Hall."

"That's a lie," Amy insisted. "Luigi would never do that."

Dennis was even more angry than Amy. "It's Grainger!" he told the others. "He said he'd get Luigi.

Now he's done it! We've got to do something."

"No!" said Norman. "We promised Mike we'd leave it to him."

Dennis was disgusted. "Mike!" he hissed. "We don't even know if he's doing anything."

But Dennis had no need to worry. Because at that moment Mike Johnson and two American soldiers were waiting outside a telephone box in the village. Inside the box, Vivienne Belling was speaking urgently into the mouthpiece.

"The message is – I have all the information. Including photographs. Be ready for action any time." She looked pleased with herself as she put the 'phone down. She wasn't so pleased when she turned round and found three soldiers waiting outside.

———>•<———

At Westbourne Hall, the telephone rang. Grainger picked it up.

He listened for a moment. A look of panic spread across his face. "What do you think you're doing telephoning me?" he snapped. There was a brief pause. "I don't care what's cropped up he," he said. "And tonight's out of the question." His face was growing red with anger. "That's your problem," he shouted into the mouthpiece. "I've told you we can't . . ." But the line had gone dead.

He turned to Millington in despair. "It's tonight," he said.

Outside the door, Mary had heard everything. She grinned to herself. Things were definitely on the move.

———>•<———

At Wells Farm, Norman, Polly and Dennis were waiting. It was as though everything had come to a stop. They couldn't do anything until they heard from Mike Johnson. And Mike seemed to be taking for ever.

Then suddenly, his jeep was roaring up to the gate.

As soon as the children saw the look on Mike's face, they knew that something was wrong.

"Did you get her?" Polly asked. "What's happened?"

Mike took a deep breath. "Look guys," he told them. "This is not going to be easy for you. You're going to have to trust me, OK?"

There was an uneasy silence. Polly, Norman and Dennis didn't know what to expect. What came next was as bad as could be.

"Forget about spies!" said Mike. "Forget about Vivienne Belling. Forget about Grainger. Keep well away from Westbourne Hall."

Norman was amazed. He couldn't believe what he was hearing.

"What do you mean?" he said.

"Just take my word," said Mike. "That's what you have to do. And listen – this is an order!"

It was the biggest blow yet. Hopes had been so high. Now it looked as though Mike had deserted them. They went to bed that night in a state of shock. They couldn't think what to do next. They didn't have to wait long before that problem was solved for them.

It was hardly dark when a handful of gravel clattered against the window. It was Mary.

"Come on!" she called up to them. "It's now!"

Chapter 10
CAPTURED

In no time at all, Norman, Dennis and Polly were out in the farmyard.

"Come on!" Mary whispered. "We've got to hurry. The lorries went down there half an hour ago."

Mary seemed to have no fear at all. The thought of getting her own back on Grainger and Millington was driving her forward.

Norman, Polly and Dennis weren't quite so brave. In the dark of night, everything seemed more dangerous. More threatening. The mist was growing thicker all the time. They would have turned back but Mary kept urging them on.

At last, they were looking down into the quarry from above. Lights had been rigged up. Two lorries were there. A gang of men were unloading boxes from one of them. Millington was checking off the boxes on a list while Grainger bustled around telling everybody what to do.

As the boxes came off the lorry, they were taken up the tunnel to Westbourne Hall. It was too far away to see what was in the boxes. But one thing was certain – it wasn't guns.

"They're not heavy enough!" Dennis whispered.

"What is in them then?" Polly wondered.

They soon found out. One of the men dropped a box as he was sliding it off the lorry. It crashed to the ground.

"Watch what you're doing!" Millington snapped. "We're not paying for anything broken."

"Very sorry!" the man sneered. "I didn't realise stockings and soap broke so easily!"

"Perhaps not," Grainger warned him. "But there's perfume in some of these. And cigarettes. So just be careful!"

So that was it. The lorries were loaded with goods for the black market. Grainger and Millington were buying up things that were in short supply and selling them again at a huge profit. Some of the boxes had US Army marks on them. They had been stolen from the base.

The children slid back from the edge. Now they knew exactly what was going on, they were disappointed.

"So they're not spies then," Dennis complained.

"Just crooks!" said Polly.

But Mary wasn't going to let that spoil things. "It's still against the law," she pointed out. "They'll go to prison if they're caught."

The thought of Grainger and Millington in prison made everyone feel a little better.

"We've got to get the police," said Norman.

"How?" asked Polly. "They'll probably be gone by the time we get to the telephone box."

But Mary had already thought of that. "We won't go to the telephone box. We'll telephone from the Hall. There's nobody there."

Polly grinned. Mary was right. "Come on!" she said.

But before Polly had gone more than half a dozen steps, her foot disappeared into a pothole and she fell to the ground. "Owww! My ankle!" she yelled. The pain was agonising.

Dennis and Norman helped her up. But it was no good. She could barely walk. She would slow them down too much.

Norman made a decision. "You and Dennis stay here. I'll go with Mary to telephone."

Polly didn't like it. But there was no other way. "All right then," she said. "But hurry up!"

⟹•⟸

Polly wasn't the only person with a problem. Down in the quarry, Grainger was struggling to untie the canvas sheet that was covering the second lorry's load.

"Hurry up! We haven't got all night," Millington was getting jumpy. The sooner the lorries were unloaded and away, the better.

Grainger tugged at the rope with all his might but it was stuck fast.

"Cut it," Millington snapped.

"Nobody's got a knife!" said Grainger.

"Don't you think of anything?" Millington sighed. She stalked off towards the tunnel. "I'll go and get one."

Norman and Mary slipped into Westbourne Hall through a side door.

Mary led the way through to the dining room. She picked up the telephone receiver.

"What do I say?" she asked Norman.

Norman tried to think. "Get the operator. Ask for the police. Tell them to get to Westbourne Quarry straight away."

Still Mary wasn't sure. Why would the police take any notice of what she said?

"Tell them you're Miss Millington," Norman said.

"But that's a lie!" A woman's voice cut through the air.

Mary turned.

Millington was standing in the doorway. She had a kitchen knife in her hand. "Put the telephone down," she growled.

Mary shook her head.

Millington edged forward. "Just do what I tell you," she hissed. "Put the telephone down."

Mary started to replace the handset. Then she stopped. "No!" she told Millington. "I'm not doing anything else you say." Mary was not going to give up. Not now they were so close to winning.

But Millington had a plan. She crouched down and grabbed the telephone wire. In one quick movement of her hand, she sliced through the wire with the knife.

As she did it, Mary hurled the telephone at her. Millington fell back in surprise. It was all Mary and Norman needed.

They raced into the hall and headed for the back door.

They didn't get far. Grainger was blocking the way. He reached out and grabbed Mary. "What's going on?" he snarled.

Mary's reply was instant. She kicked Grainger's shin as hard as she could.

Grainger doubled over in pain.

"The front!" shouted Mary.

Norman and Mary ran back towards the front doors. Millington was on her way out of the dining room. She dived at Mary but Mary dodged sideways and Millington crashed to the floor again. Grainger had recovered from Mary's kick and was racing after them. Millington slid straight into his legs and he tumbled down on top of her.

Norman and Mary reached the front entrance while Grainger and Millington were still picking themselves up. Mary grabbed the door handle and twisted it. The handle turned but the door stayed firmly shut. It was locked. There was no way out.

Grainger and Millington had trapped them. This time there was no escape.

"Something's wrong. They should be back by now."
Polly was worried. Norman and Mary had been away
too long.

Dennis was peering down into the quarry. "Wait!" he
said. "There's something happening."

Polly scrambled forward to see what was going on.
What she saw took her breath away. Grainger and
Millington were marching Norman and Mary across the
quarry towards an old shed. Grainger opened the door
and pushed the children inside. Then he fastened the
door shut.

"They'll be all right there for a bit," he told
Millington. "Now come on."

Grainger started to move away but Millington
grabbed his arm.

"We can't leave it like that," she hissed. "They know
too much. We've got to deal with them."

"Don't be stupid," Grainger scoffed.

But Millington was deadly serious. "What's your
idea?" she asked. "Let them go? To put us in jail?"

Grainger was worried now. "Look," he said. "What
we're doing is against the law. But nobody gets hurt."

"There's no other way," Millington insisted. "There'll
be no problem. It'll look like an accident. Two kids
messing around in a quarry at night. Very dangerous."

Grainger pulled his arm free and started to walk
away. "I've told you – no!" he said.

But Millington wasn't going to give up. "We'll sort it
out later," she said.

Dennis and Polly had to do something if Norman and Mary were to have any chance. But what?

Polly struggled to her feet. "I think I can get down to the telephone box by the bridge," she told Dennis. Her ankle was still painful but she would just have to forget about it.

Dennis nodded. "Do that!" he said. "I'm going down into the quarry."

———➤●◄———

The gang had started to unload the second lorry. Even Grainger was helping, trying to keep away from Millington. But as he pulled a box down she caught up with him.

"Those kids!" she hissed. "What if the other two are around somewhere?"

"You think you're the only one with any brains?" Grainger sneered. "I've already sent somebody to look for them."

———➤●◄———

Polly hobbled painfully along the track towards the lane. Suddenly, a torch was shining straight into her eyes. Somebody was blocking the way. But Polly was too dazzled to see who.

A woman's voice broke the silence. "You! Don't you ever give up?"

It was Vivienne Belling. "You really are a bit of a nuisance," Belling continued.

Polly had never been so angry. Nobody was going to stop her now. Especially not Vivienne Belling. She hurled herself forward in a mad rage. "And you're a dirty rotten spy!" she yelled.

Her hands grabbed Belling's hair. She pulled with all her might.

Belling screamed. "Get her off, will you?"

Somebody grabbed Polly from behind and dragged her away. "Polly! It's OK. It's me!"

It was Mike Johnson.

Polly stared at him in amazement. What was going on? "What are you doing here?" she demanded.

Mike ignored the question. "The others!" he said. "Where are they?"

"Down at the quarry," Polly answered. "They got caught."

"We've got to get in there at top speed," Mike told Belling.

Belling signalled along the track with her torch. Engines started up, then army vehicles and a police car roared down the track.

As they skidded into the quarry, the men who were unloading the lorries scattered in every direction. They had no chance of escape – they were outnumbered two to one by soldiers and policemen.

Millington turned towards the shed. "The kids!" she shouted to Grainger. "Get hold of those kids!"

But Grainger had had enough. He blocked the way. "Leave them!" he ordered.

"Never!" Millington pushed him over and sprinted towards the shed. Grainger picked himself up and charged after her.

Millington raced inside the shed with Grainger hot on her heels. They stopped dead. The shed was empty. They turned only to see Mary slam the door shut on them. They stared at each other in horror. Now they were caught.

Outside, Norman and Mary grinned at Dennis. He had got to them just in time.

It had been a night to remember. A night where everything had turned out right in the end. But only just. Now they had some explaining to do.

<hr />

The next day, the Wells Farm kitchen was packed with people. Amy was run off her feet, trying to keep everybody supplied with tea and toast.

"Lucky to be alive! All of them!" said Amy. She still hadn't recovered from the shock.

Vivienne Belling smiled. "They did a good job though. After all, they weren't to know that I was after Grainger as well."

Norman, Polly and Dennis were just a bit embarrassed. They had got it all wrong. Vivienne Belling wasn't a spy, after all. She was working for the Government, trying to track down people who were running the black market.

"And catching black marketeers is very nearly as good as catching a spy!" Belling told Polly.

Mike Johnson agreed. "They did a darn good job," he said.

It was true. They had done a darned good job. But now it had come to an end. Especially for Norman and Dennis. They were going home.

Their parents had decided that the countryside was too dangerous. It was safer in the city after all.

Mr Jenkins was taking Dennis back. And Mrs Starkey had come to collect Norman.

Only Mary was staying behind.

"I telephoned her parents and told them what had happened to her," Mr Jenkins said to Mike Johnson as he loaded Dennis's things into his car. "And they just asked me to find her somewhere else to stay." Mr Jenkins shook his head in wonder.

"I've told you, Cyril Jenkins. That girl's staying here with me and Polly," said Amy. Amy was in no mood for arguing. Mary needed looking after and she was going to do it.

Mrs Starkey climbed into Mike Johnson's jeep. It was time for her and Norman to go.

"Thank you for everything, Mrs Hobbs," she said to Amy.

"No thanks necessary," Amy was fighting back the tears. She grabbed Norman and Dennis and hugged them till they could barely breathe.

Norman climbed into the back seat of the jeep. Mrs Starkey sat in front. Mike Johnson started the engine. He pushed the gear lever forward and the jeep moved off across the farmyard.

Mary ran after them. "Norman, your gas mask!"

"Give it to Dennis," shouted Norman.

"Give it to the goat!" Dennis replied.

Everybody laughed. But behind the laughter there was sadness.

Norman looked back. Polly, Dennis, Mary and Amy were waving goodbye. Norman waved. And he kept waving until Wells Farm was out of sight.

It had only been his home for a few weeks. But he'd remember it for the rest of his life.